5-14-16

the author's table

Thank you
for your support.

Peace & Love

Dianne

2

Cruisin'

and Other Short Stories

Cruisin'

and Other Short Stories

by

Dianne Gill

D. James Publishing, LLC

P.O. Box 4246

Hartford, CT   06147-4246

djamespublishingllc.com

Cover design - Young Studios - 2012

Edited by Kimberly James - 2012

First printing 2012

ISBN 978-0-9847513-1-0

LCCN 2012907274

First Edition

10 9 8 7 6 5 4 3 2 1

The people, places, and events, in this book are all created from my imagination with no reflection whatsoever on my personal life or the life of my family and friends.

Acknowledgements

I want to thank God first for giving me the thoughts and talent to get this all down on paper. Thank you to my Husband, Morgan "Fella" Gill who never laughed at my dreams. My Son Quincey (QQ my Baby), My Step Son's Morgan Jr., Davon and Andre (Dre aka Amazin) who all show love all the time. Thanks to my first Original Editors! My sisters Linda and Paula and Sister Friend Kim (Kimmie Hall James), cuz Wanda and Aset, Big thanks to my Mom Barbara and my Dad Horace for raising us to stand up for ourselves, never judging and always giving an honest opinion. My sisters, Paula, Linda, Carole, Gail, Lu Ann (wat up Lauren ☺), and my Brother Bruce for understanding and being there for me. Thank you to my sister in law Laura and her family, and my brother in Law Sam and his family thank you to all my nieces and nephews, Tracy, Chris, Jennifer, Robert (Bam), Brandee, Justin, James, Lily, Olivia, Bruce Jr, for always showing love. Thank you to my wonderful in-laws, Marjorie and Monroe (Mom and Dad) Rocky (Roxanne), Senita, Natasha and Tenika, Stacy and Mark, Monroe (Fuddy).... all of ya'll and so many more I can't even name, please forgive me if I missed your name. Oh can't leave out my daughter in laws..love ya'll Nik (Nikaya) and Barbara. Big Thank you to my mentor and Awesome cover designer Joe Young, Jr. and Kyle Young of Young studios. Thank you for the encouragement and guidance and thank you for forever keeping it real with me. Thanks to my Attorney Tom McNeill, Jr. Tom, thanks for being patient with me. Cuz Ja Vision Enterprises LLC for hooking up my Website Thanks Cuz!!Thank you to my BFF's Amie W, Wanda M, Carol S and her family, Thank you, Peace and love to you all.

Table of Contents

Cruisin'

Cruisin'

Chapter One

1.

"Life is too short. I have to stop talking about it and start being about it."

Vevee thought to herself while she clicked around online looking for that perfect trip to take her away from it all. On her sorority website, she came across a travel agency.

She clicked on the link and printed off the website information. Once she had it in her hand she reviewed it a little closer.

It was a picture of an athletic looking sister with long pretty auburn color dreds in a red bikini. The model in the ad was being served a cocktail with an umbrella in it by a light brown caramel skinned brother wearing white shorts and muscles to die for. Vevee took the ad, picked up a pen off her desk and walked over to the sitting area in the one bedroom apartment.

She plopped down on her favorite overstuffed, forest green loveseat that was covered with a soft, flannel like material.

Bright colorful pillows of greens, blues, and reds were tossed on it. She got comfortable and stared closer at the ad.

Call today to reserve a spot on our Singles Weekend Cruise..$695.00...Includes Air Fare and Meals.

"Oh, Vevee talked softly to herself, "I can afford that."

She let her mind wander while she stared at the advertisement in front of her. Vevee pictured herself in a red bikini soaking up the sun while her ex-boyfriend rubbed her shoulders. She sat up abruptly and rubbed her temples.

"I have to forget about that loser, time to move on."

With that thought, she grabbed the cordless phone and dialed the 800 number to the travel agency.

17

Vevee

Arriving in sunny Miami from her cold, dreary state of Connecticut, Vevee felt an adrenalin rush while she exited the plane. She sensed eyes following her while she strutted towards baggage claim.

Vevee was happy that she packed light and only had one bag to collect off the rounder. Out of the corner of her eye, she could see the man that was on the plane, seated a few seats back from her. His eyes were following her.

She placed her carryon, a big Luis Vuitton duffle bag at her feet, unzipped the top and pretended to look for something.

Usually pretty conservative in her attire, Vevee had spiced up her wardrobe especially for this trip. She was wearing a loose fitting yellow silk halter top, a shape hugging jean skirt that stopped right before her knees and 3 inch Joan & David canvas open toe slides with blue and yellow strips.

"Work it girl," she thought to herself while she smiled and enjoyed the attention.

She thought her stalling to look in her bag would give him time to approach her. When she turned toward him and smiled, he quickly looked away. Oh well, Vevee thought, shy type.

Veeve had spotted three and a possible 4th man on her flight that she thought were heading for the cruise. Two very good looking and two very average looking. The man staring at her was one of the good looking ones.

She recalled a conversation she had with her best friend Mandi. Mandi had warned her before she left,

"Just because it's a singles cruise, don't mean everyone there is single. Don't let them men fool you girl, be careful."

"Well I'm going to enjoy the sun and service, forget them damn men for one weekend." she reassured her girl.

"If I see a hot one, I might play a little, but I ain't getting all wrapped up, I'm trying to relax. I might use my fake name."

Vevee laughed into the phone and hung up with Mandi.

Vevee was deep in thought while she waited for her bag. Her cell phone rang bringing her out of her daydream. It was her mother on the other end.

Vevee went on to answer all her mother's questions.

"Yeah Ma, I'm fine. I have my hair up in a
bun. I didn't want to wait to get all those
braids.

No, I can still swim, I just won't go under.
No Ma, it looks very classy. I left the travel
itinerary with Vindy."

Her Mom was into V names. Her sister was
Vindy, her brother Victor and hers was
Vaveetta. God how she hated that name, but
she didn't mind Vevee which was what
everyone called her.

"O.K. Ma, love you to, I'll call you when I
get home."

She ended her call and spotted her bag.
Vevee grabbed her bag off the rounder and
started towards the shuttle bus area. While
waiting to speak with one of the airport
attendees for directions, she spotted the

same good looking man from the plane
staring at her.

She gave him a quick once over and admired
his brown leather sandals, olive linen
drawstring pants, and loose fitting linen shirt
that showed off his flat stomach. She made
eye contact, he smiled, and she smiled back.
Vevee was feeling free as a bird, forgetting
all her troubles.
The man in the blue airport uniform with
matching hat asked
 "May I help you Miss?"

She turned her attention to him and asked
what time her shuttle would arrive and
where she should wait. The short shuttle
ride to the cruise ship would be in less than
thirty minutes.

He suggested she wait at a small eatery in
the corner and then at about twenty after, get
in line under the blue shuttle to ship sign.

23

Vevee thanked him and looked back towards where she saw her admirer. He was gone.

She walked back to the eatery and ordered a small French vanilla coffee. She sat and relaxed her feet. While contemplating meeting the handsome man on the plane she thumbed through the latest Essence magazine. She would take it slow, she told herself. Just some fun and sun.

Chapter Two

2.

Dallen

Dallen grinned to himself while he walked out of the airport to the drop off area. He found an empty bench next to an ashtray. He pulled out his cigarette and lit it.

"This is going to be easy this time," he thought to himself.

Miss thing was already smiling and flirting. Women always came easy to him. He pictured himself as quite the ladies man.

Dallen was even named that in his high school year book. Women were one thing in his life that came easy.

He contemplated his next move while he smoked. She was a naïve one, starved for attention. He could tell by the way she showed him her ass while bending and looking in her bag. Little did she know he was peeping her big Louis Vuitton, it was real and screamed working girl on it! Dallen could spot a woman with money a mile away and he was right on target. He noticed her whole outfit, from the top to the shoes; he could almost smell the designer newness of them. He also noticed the tight body. Definite gym membership or personal trainer, he thought.

No broke broad would have it together like little miss career women. He knew her type well.

Her face was ok, a little plain; he sized her up, more homely than cute. The homely ones were always a little more grateful. Dallen reasoned that would work to his advantage. He was always known as a pretty boy and worked it for all it was worth.

Dallen flagged a cab, jumped in it and directed the driver to the docking area.

He learned on his last trip that the cab was fifteen dollars cheaper than the shuttle. He maxed the last five hundred dollars on his credit card to go on the trip. He was depending on the $100.00 in twenties in his pocket to get him through the trip.

He would attempt to pay the gratuities in advance with his maxed out card, this usually worked.

The credit card company would let it go on his card and charge him ridiculous overage fees. Dallen didn't have time to worry about overage fees.

"One hundred bucks along with my charm and good looks, I should make it o.k.," he thought to himself.

Dallen had been on the cruise 3 years in a row and it was beginning to be a habit. He was tired of running his hustle. But the same time each year, he found himself in need of money and itching to get away. The cruise hustle scratched his itch.

Dallen looked forward to the day when he could book a family cruise instead of this singles one.

He would give his latest cruise conquest his best shot at a long term relationship.

"Maybe she will be the one", Dallen thought while he tried to rid himself of that familiar depressing feeling he got right before he tricked and deceived his target.

A loose long distance relationship would prove successful to Dallen. He wouldn't mind traveling out of town every once in a while to spend time with that special someone.

Dallen thought of his last failed relationship and tried to focus on the business at hand.

"I need to come up with the rent for next month and at least some get by money,"

Dallen worked intently on a list of bills he wrote on the small pad he carried in his travel bag.

"If I get her into my bed, at least I have a chance at sneaking one of her credit cards. That way, even if I have to charge up a bunch of items from one of the ships boutiques I could sell it on the street."

Dallen thought to himself while he went through his list of bills. He also planned to have her mind completely occupied and off such trivial matters, and completely absorbed with him. That was what worked for him and that was what he was good at.

Dallen knew that after all the guests got acclimated with the ship and the schedule of events, people would loosen up and get to drinking and eating.

Since it was a singles cruise, he hoped there would be more than that one women he marked at the dock to pay him some attention and maybe start a long term relationship. At least he could get a couple of month's companionship out of the deal. He realized he was getting older and not younger and didn't want to be left lonely like many of his uncles he was raised around.

His uncles had lived fast and free when it came to women.

Dallen had memories of riding in their new cars and picking up different women to take them for a ride around town. They would pick up their nephew little D, as they use to call him, and put him in the back.

As he grew older, he learned that his Uncles were using him to have an easy out with the women who demanded rides to the grocery store or the laundry mat. Every time they would say, "I have to drop little D back off or you know I would take you," or "I can drop you but sure can't come back and pick you up because I need to spend time with my Nephew."

Dallen had fond memories of those days.
He learned that deceiving women was easy
and accepted among the men in his family.

Dallen hit the pool area so he could see what
he had to work with. 4 fats, 1 to damn
skinny, 2 lesbians,

 "Aren't they on the wrong cruise?" he
thought to himself.

And to his delight 1 dime along with a not
so bad looking friend. They caught his eye
while he walked around and flashed a smile.
They both smiled back at him.

He saw the same women from earlier on the dock and she was looking hot. A bright red bikini along with a white sheer cover-up showed her flawless complexion and toned body.

He stared and smiled at her when she finally felt him staring and turned in his direction. She smiled back and pretended to look at a magazine while she posed poolside in a chaise lounge.

"I'll start with this one, and take one at a time," Dallen had a good feeling about this and relaxed.

He took a seat at a table on the far side of the deck.

Out of the corner of his eye he saw the drummer from the ships band, Morgan with the dreds.

He hustled the women passengers in the same manner as Dallen. They had bumped heads in the past; Dallen had to put him in his place.

He convinced Morgan that they both could benefit by acting like they didn't know each other instead of bitching up like Morgan did on one of the previous cruises.

Dallen was working on one of the more cautious, conservative passengers. She wasn't a big drinker and Dallen was having a hard time getting her to relax and trust him. Morgan spoke with the women and gave out his real name and the number of times he had seen Dallen on the cruise in the past. The name part didn't matter to Dallen. He changed his name every time he boarded.

It was the number of times he had been on board that he couldn't explain to the young, pretty socialite.

He was furious when she started questioning him and even asked to see his ID. He had to let her go and make himself scarce the rest of the cruise.

Dallen caught up to Morgan when they boarded in Miami. Morgan was kissing a young mixed looking women and a small boy goodbye. Dallen was surprised to see he was involved. It made him dislike Morgan. He figured if he had a family, the last thing he would do is go dicking around on a cruise ship for kicks.

He struck up a conversation with Morgan and offered to buy him a drink before boarding.

Morgan looked suspicious at first, then he glanced over at the bar area with a young white bartender. She had long dark hair to her waist, pulled back by a blue head band, to match her low cut blue tee shirt, exposing large D cups atop her tight black jeans. She was smiling and mixing drinks, chatting with the patrons.

Dallen and Morgan took a seat and Morgan was quick to order a top shelf drink while Dallen stuck to a domestic beer. Dallen mentioned the previous situation with the socialite; he mentioned his cousin who worked as an immigration officer and a gang affiliated brother who didn't have a problem making people disappear.

Morgan got the message loud and clear.
Although Dallen was exaggerating the facts,
Morgan didn't know that and didn't need
any trouble, with all the dirt he was doing.
Now when they saw each other on the
cruise, they didn't even give the customary
nod that brothers do.

Chapter Three

3.

Dallen

Dallen didn't mind the competition. These cruises had enough women for every player, hustler and pimp. Even the real man looking to get romantically involved could pick and choose.

Over the years that he had been running his hustle, he would run into the women on board who had been on the cruise once or twice before. He wondered if these women were unlucky in love, or were they running game like him.

Also a board were the working girls, they weren't hard to spot. Scantily clad, heavily made up and usually at the Captains table. He couldn't knock their hustle. Morgan the dred was into the white women. That was fine with him. While Dallen didn't think of his self as prejudiced, he preferred the sisters. He felt a connection with them and in the back of his heart and mind, he knew he wanted stability and a good relationship with a strong black women. There was nothing like it.

The waiter came by and bought him out of his daydream, and he glanced over at the women of his interest.

He saw her drink was empty on the side
table.

Thinking about his limited funds, he peeled
a twenty off of the 4 he had in his pocket,
checked his breath and said a quick prayer
that this would swing his way. His money
was on low and he didn't want to waste time
and money, especially money.

Dallen ordered 2 margaritas and when they
came he approached her lounge chair.

"Good afternoon beautiful," Dallen smiled
looking down at the woman.

He looked into her eyes trying hard not to let
them wander down her taut body. The white
cover-up had slid open and her long brown
leg was bent resting on the other.

He gave her his best smile.

"My name is Dallen and I was wondering if I could join you?" he gestured at the empty lounge chair next to her.

Vevee squinted up at this handsome specimen.

"Took him long enough," she thought to herself.

She sat up and took the drink he handed her.

"Sure, she said, "Make yourself comfortable. My name is Vevee, nice to meet you Dallen."

Vevee gave her best smile back at him.

Chapter Four

4.

Vevee

"Woooo, I'm telling you, you shoulda came baby girl."

Vevee talked into her cell phone to her friend Mandi back home. She twirled in front of the mirror over her small dresser in the small cabin.

"I'm wearing a black silk number I picked up from one of the stores here. Girl, it's like a freakin mall on this big mother."

Vevee had chosen a sexy but slightly conservative St. John dress to go out with her date she met while sitting poolside, Dallen.

"It's not sleazy," she explained to Mandi.

"Some of these hoe's are just plain ridiculous out here, they don't have on NO clothes," she emphasized the word no.

"I don't want ol'boy to get the wrong idea."

"Girl, you know your going to let him hit it, I don't know why your playin," Mandi laughed.

"Well I like him to think he has to work at it anyway," Vevee laughed back.

"Let me go," Mandi said, "Someone's at my door, talk to you when you get home and Ve, have fun but BE SAFE!"

Vevee brushed back a few strays from her bun and looked approvingly at herself.

"The hair looks right, the body tight, I'm Hot all night."

Vevee felt light headed and she didn't know if it was from the constant flow of mimosa's and champagne the ship provided, or the anticipation of a roll in the hay with a perfect stranger. She sprayed on her favorite sent and started off towards the lounge where she and Dallen agreed to meet.

Chapter Five

5.

Dallen

Dallen pulled out his dry cleaned suit. He had one last linen short outfit to wear for the final day on the ship. He would chill in his cabin and bypass all the black tie crap that was on the ships social agenda. He showered and changed.

Looking in the mirror before he left, Dallen thought to himself, "I still got it," he turned to check his profile. His dark dreamy eyes and fresh hair cut complimented his smooth skin.

He had his mustache trimmed neat and it was hard for people to tell his age. Although he didn't have what you called a "baby face", something about his eyes and his swagger was full of mischief and very youthful.

He would never admit to being over 40. He told most women he was 36 or 39. This seemed to be a believable age, for someone with no wife, or steady job to converse about.

He simply stuck to the story that he is coming off a bad breakup, and had never been married.

When asked, he said he worked construction with a company that put up new sub developments. This seemed to work every time so he stuck with variations of the story.

He sat on the edge of the bed and an overwhelming feeling of exhaustion and sadness filled him. He laid straight back on the bed and closed his eyes. In his head he went over the steps that led him where he was now in his life.

Being born an only child, his mother protected him and kept him sheltered well into his teens.

His parents Tessa and El were high school sweethearts. His father, was a strict, no nonsense man who worked at a local garage.

The garage closed in the 80's due to the introduction of chains like "Jiffy Lube" and El went to work a late shift as an attendant in a parking garage. Both his parents were good looking Black people.

His Mom, Tessa, kept a short cut that complimented her big brown eyes and dimples. Her naturally curly hair framed her round face. She had a petite frame with curves in the right places. His Dad, El, had dark smooth chocolate skin and shiny black eyes that were slanted, some might say "tight."

This gave him an exotic sort of look. Tall and strong from doing physical labor from the age of 15, he was in great shape for a man his age.

His Grandmother on his Mom's side, was said to have a line of Indian blood, from a tribe who claimed land in the Massachusetts area. His Father's people were from the west coast whose skin complexion ranged from light, bright almost white, to dark as your shoe black.

No one ever explained to Dallen what they were mixed with. Traces of mixed blood from his ancestors were obvious.

"What Are You?"

He always got that question, sometimes right when he met someone, or sometimes the person would wait until they felt comfortable enough to ask. Dallen fell somewhere in the middle of the range.

He was brown, like a cinnamon stick and red when he got a tan in the summer. His hair was wavy but not curly like his Mom's. His eyes were tight like his Dad's and he inherited his mom's dimples.

Dallen had pleasant childhood memories of playing with neighborhood friends, never needing food, clothes or shelter.

He didn't feel rich, like the white kids at his school who got dropped off by nannies, or poor, like the foster kids who had to wear the same three pair of pants to school the whole school year, just comfortably in the middle. One thing he remembered being most proud of was having his Dad and Mom together in the same house.

Unlike most of the neighborhood kids he ran with, his Dad was there when he went to sleep and when he woke up.

Things got rocky between his parents when his Dad changed jobs and began to hang out with the "late shift crowd" as his Mom put it. Dallen's Mom worked off and on odd jobs, sometimes at the strip mall up the street from the house in a retail store called Barbara's Backroom.

It sold designer suits and dresses that were from the previous season. Tessa could fit all of the petite styles and would buy 2 or 3 suits or dresses at a time when they went on sale.

When that store went out of business, his Mom would put on one of her designer dresses, 3 inch heels and go down to Main street to one of the black owned bars and bartend. Like in most towns, all the black owned businesses were located on a few consecutive blocks in the bad part of town. Main Street held all of the Black, West Indian, Caribbean American, and Puerto Rican businesses.

Like most towns, they consisted of package stores, bars, bodegas, not to exclude the Chinese takeout and nail joints separated by churches.

Tessa was a great bartender and would talk mess with the best of them, never to be backed down by a drunken customer or a jealous wife who came cussing her when they couldn't find their husband.

Dallen remembered sitting in the vinyl red booth with a coke soda and his comic books or Right-On magazines. This is where he learned to study women. He watched his mom play men for big tips, leaning over the bar and smiling.

She would clean up on tips sometimes bringing home one-hundred dollars a night, which back then was like three hundred.

When his dad worked the night shift at the garage, which included many weekends, he would accompany his mom to the bar from time to time. She didn't feel comfortable leaving him in the house by himself.

At twelve years old, he felt strange seeing his mom smile and flirt with all the men at the bar. She stopped bringing him all together after a valentine's weekend he would never forget.

Shayvon was a regular at the bar. Every time he was with his mom, she would sashay over to the booth and lean into the table. Dallen's mom would glance back at them over her shoulder and address Shayvon,

"Watch yourself miss thing, he is still a minor."

Dallen recognized the tone his mom reserved for the regulars that knew her but didn't really know her. It was playful yet serious.

Tessa or Ms. T was what most of the people from the bar called her. His mom knew how to draw the line, especially with the drunk or about to be drunk patrons.

"How you doin Shorty,?" letting her breasts hang in her low cut shirt, Dallen grinned looking up at her from his magazine.

He was nervous but at the same time in awe. No one ever called him "Shorty." By the time he was twelve Dallen was taller then most of the kids in his class and had at least a half inch on Shayvone.

Shayvone was the first women he ever saw with a gold tooth in the front of her mouth. His mom always said everything that's new is old. She also explained to him that a lot of the fashion statements that his generation sported, came from back in the day out of plain necessity.

"If you had a gold tooth, it was because you probably had a little money but a country ass dentist. Back in the day, not all the good dentists were seeing black folk. We had to go to certain ones. Gold wasn't meant to go in your mouth; it eventually will rot your teeth."

That particular evening Shayvon was feeling good because it was Valentine's Day and she had a new ring from her man and a few drinks before she hit the bar.

She explained all this to Dallen while she cozied up to him in the booth. Every few minutes she would glance at his mom to make sure she was still busy and not paying attention.

Dallen didn't mind the attention. Shayvon wasn't what you called pretty, but she smelled good to Dallen. Like a mix of vanilla and hairspray. He loved looking at her breasts. Her gold jewelry always hung way down into her shirts and her tight cloths made him get a hard on at night when he thought about her.

While she was talking she rested her hand on his thigh under the table. Dallen felt heat from her hand and the fire move up into his groin.

Shayvon rested her elbow on the table, slightly turning her back to the bar area. This blocked his mothers view of him. Shayvon rubbed his thigh back and forth and Dallen let her. She stopped once to use the ladies room. The bar was so crowded at that point, he could barely see his mom when she came to the end of the bar that was closest to him. Shayvon came back laughing loud with a drink in her hand. She gave Dallen the once over with her glazed eyes.

"Now, where were we Shorty?" as she sat back down next to him.

She took the same position, turning her back slightly to the bar and put her hand on his leg. This time she stroked all the way up and grabbed his dick. Dallen's eyes almost popped out his head. No women had ever touched him there.

The most action he got was from slutty
Sylvia at school who was letting boys grind
her in the corner for $1 for 5 minutes.
Drunk Shayvon rubbed and stroked and
Dallen sat still and enjoyed. One of the
other patrons came over to the booth,
startling both of them out of their private
involvement.

 "Girl this Ms. T's son? He done got big for
sure! Why you look so scared baby?" she
looked at his eyes popping out his head.

Her eyes followed Shayvon's arm under the
table and she said in a loud, drunk voice

"What ya doin' to that boy Shayvon?" The
next thing he remembers was seeing
Shayvon fall backwards out of the booth and
his mother snatching him up out of it.

She stepped over Shayvon who was scrambling to get up and go after the women who had bought the attention to her little private party. His mom grabbed his coat and his magazines and stomped out of the bar with him by the arm. That was the last time he accompanied his mom to work.

Dallen sat up and laughed to himself at the memory. He hit the shower in preparation for his date. The hot water felt good as it washed over him changing his mood from sad to mellow. He hoped that maybe his latest conquest could end up being more than a temporary fix.

Chapter Six

6.

Vevee

After a night of dinner and dancing, and drinking, Vevee was more than lightheaded, she was straight drunk.

Looking at Dallen she felt she was ready to throw caution to the wind. She had 3 condoms in her little silver clutch and was ready to go for it.

Dancing with Dallen all night and rubbing up against him while slow dancing was All the foreplay she needed to decide if she was going to get a little closer to Dallen or put things on stall till tomorrow.

She sized up the competition while they were at dinner. Vevee caught a few of the women staring at her and Dallen and some even boldly flirting with her date. He smiled at all the women but was a gentleman to her and didn't disrespect her.

There was a moment when she felt she was going to have to get "ugly" on him. He left the dinner table to go to the men's room and a blond that had been staring got up and followed him from the next table over.

The blonde was sitting with a few other women and one man, who judging from his shoes, haircut and really manicured eyebrows, was possibly gay. The blonde brushed by Dallen and said something to him. Vevee could see Dallen stop and smile and say something back. This bold bitch touched his arm and continued to talk to him.

Dallen must have felt her eyes burning him, he glanced back at the table, and side stepped to get the blonde off his arm, and kept it moving to the men's room.

"These women are too much", Vevee thought to herself.

Vevee didn't want to take a chance of turning Dallen down tonight, playing Ms. Good Girl and losing him to one of the hoes, who would surely pick him up, eat him up and may not turn him loose until the end of the cruise.

There was only one other guy who could be a possible prospect for a good time on the ship. He started a quick conversation with her when she was browsing in one of the 5 boutiques on the ship.

Cute enough but rough around the edges, Vevee felt safer getting to know Dallen. He seemed like a little older, working class guy. Although she couldn't call it, there was something a little shady about Dallen.

He didn't want to talk about his job or his college life or anything of that nature. That was fine with Vevee at this point. She wasn't trying to get married and had seen on Oprah, never, ever bring up your ex to a possible next. So their conversation was limited to the here and now.

After the last dance, Dallen held her around the waist and offered her one last drink. The bar had made the announcement of "last call."

"One for the road," Dallen smiled while speaking softly in her ear.

His arms felt strong and warm. His tight body felt damn good to Vevee and she leaned hard into his chest.

She sat back into the full backed, padded bar stool that was more like a lounge chair. Dallen ordered 2 more glasses of champagne and stood close next to her seat.

"So am I walking you back to your room or do you want to come and stay in mine?" Dallen asked her.

This caught Vevee off guard but she appreciated his straight forwardness. Her head was starting to swim and it was definitely time for her to make a decision.

She wondered how he was holding up after all the champagne. She had never seen a man drink that much champagne and wondered was it because it was free.

After the third glass she was feeling it so she came right out and asked.

His reply, coupled with a surprised look was,

"Champagne is one of the alcohols I drink on occasion. I try not to drink at all but after meeting you, I figured I am going to celebrate the rest of my time with her on this cruise and Champagne is definitely a celebratory drink!"

Then he added

"And the fact we were given a complimentary bottle at the beginning of dinner didn't hurt either Sis."

Vevee didn't know if it was because Dallen called her "Sis" or the fact that he claimed not to be a real drinker, which had started to be a problem with her ex towards the end of their relationship.

Maybe it was the champagne itself, but whatever it was, the reply sounded refreshing and honest to her and she laughed and laughed and drank some more and laughed.

This pleased Dallen and he laughed to.

Chapter Seven

7.

Dallen

Looking at Vevee's eyes glaze over, Dallen knew he better make a move or Ol' girl was going to be sleeping in one of these bar chairs. He knew her legs were wobbly and didn't want to be seen dragging a half conscious women to his room and be questioned later in case something happened.

The less attention he attracted the better. Dallen knew that with the recent incidents of cruise ship passengers' going overboard, both figuratively and literally, the ship installed more security cameras.

She easily agreed, like he hoped, to go back to his room. They made their way to the elevator. Dallen was on the second level. In the elevator, he leaned Vevee against the wall, pushed into her and gave her a long, slow kiss. He let his hands go the length of her back, stopping just before her plump ass. He knew he was teasing her and didn't want to scare her off.

He really wanted to go up her dress and see what kind of panties she was wearing. Where they silk? He was hopping for silk, high end, with matching bra. Surely they were moist by now.

As Vevee kissed him back, she rubbed her hands through his soft hair and thought of what a good looking couple they made. She felt everything tingle and respected the fact Dallen didn't grab her ass.

Most men touched that first because it was fat and toned all at once. Dallen tasted good if a little like cigarettes.

Not overwhelming and mixed with the champagne, it was good to Vevee.

Off the elevator and into the room they held hands. Vevee was drunk but able to play it off and walk straight like she was just buzzed.

In the small cabin, Vevee plopped down on the bed. Dallen hit the small radio and soft music came on. He hit the lights next and was on top of her all in a moment. They tore at each other's clothes. She mumbled that she had condoms and he mumbled he did to. Dallen slowed it down after they were naked. He took his time and kissed Vevee everywhere, even there.

No tongue in her kitty kat, but the kisses
from his soft fat lips drove her to scream out
"Dallen Please."

He put on a condom and entered her with an
ample size dick and a strong back, turned
her over on her stomach and even smacked
her ass.

"Two times," Dallen always said, "for luck."
Pop, Vevee heard and felt a slight
stimulating sting and Smack, a hard hurt so
good smack on her ass was next. Vevee had
never been spanked before and the sensation
drove her wild. She moaned loudly. Dallen
pumped fast and hard and they climaxed
together.

Chapter Eight

8.

Vevee

When Vevee awoke, they made sweet, slow love again and Vevee even gave him some head. She sucked on top of a rubber, another thing she never did. After the second go round, Dallen told her to sleep and he would go and bring them something back to eat. She asked him why not order room service but wasn't awake or strong enough to argue when he said something like "Using all the free services he possible could."
She figured what the hell, with lovemaking like that, he could afford to be a cheap skate.

Vevee rested her head on the soft pillow and drifted off into a deep, relaxing, much needed sleep.

Dallen

Down at the first boutique Dallen purchased a silk bra and panty set in a pale yellow. He checked the size on the pale blue set crumpled next to the bed Vevee had took off to make sure he got it right.

He used the rest of his cash on this purchase, leaving himself $15.00 to get a taxi after he got off the boat.

Vevee only had an $100 bill in her clutch. He couldn't take that; it would make it to obvious.

By purchasing the bra and panty set, it would make her feel better about being so easy. This worked on most women, especially the types who were not usually loose. But when they went to a place where no one knew them, like an out of town vacation, they really let their hair down.

At the next boutique, he charged up 3 designer bags. 2 Coach and a Louis Vuitton, an expensive men's watch with bezzled diamonds around the face, and 2 pair of diamond stud earrings. One, Dallen thought to himself, will be a gift for a women back home he owed big time.

As Dallen went through his purchases in the elevator, he figured the watch would definitely make his rent. It cost $2,500.00 and he could sell it for at least $1,000.00, or $1,500.00 if he ran into one of the ballers that he knew from around the way.

With the ballers, it wasn't what he was selling or how much it cost, that mattered, it was if they were going into the clink or coming home. True ballers where always just coming home or about to go in for a short bid.

"Damn son, they would say, "I guess I'll just take those earrings for my wifey" or "Gimmee that piece for my son, let little man remember me while I'm on the inside."

That was from the ones about to go in. But from the ones just hittin bricks, just smellin the fresh air and sunshine, Dallen would always sell out. "Fuck it D, just give me the whole bag of shit man, I'm just getting out."

Once he made $5,000.00 off one bag of items that included lots of bling from a spring cruise he did really well on.

He moved out of the one bedroom he had in a rough area from the cash he made off that load. One thing about dealing with the ballers, you couldn't let them get to familiar with you because sometimes they sent their goons back to your house to take back some of the money they paid you with. Hustlers always had to stay a step ahead.

He figured he would take this life any day compared to some of the ballers who made their money from slinging drugs all day and going in and out of jail for a living.

He knew he wouldn't stand a chance in the pen. This thought made him feel tired and old.

Dallen knew he was too old to be still hustling and that this could very well lead him to prison. Dallen shifted the bags in his hands. He thought about Vevee back in the room and felt a small tinge of guilt. Maybe he should just stay in touch with Ol girl and try and make it work. He could return all the items, lie to the store clerk and say that the women he was purchasing these things for is in the room with someone else.

He had worked the sales clerks before; they were always ready for some gossip. Once he had a young lady that would give him whatever he wanted out of the boutique.

They slept together and kicked it for two days on one of the week long cruises he went on. It all ended when they reached the port of Puerto Rico and the FBI agents came and escorted Mimi off the boat in cuffs. He learned a lesson that time.

He thought he had her all figured out, running game on her, come to find out she had a lot more secrets than him to hide.

Exiting the elevator and heading down the hall to the safes, he figured he would do both with Ms.Vevee.

Today he would steal from her, but he would also make an effort to keep in touch. Easing his guilty conscious, Dallen told himself that he would make every effort to pay her back and treat her like she deserved to be treated. He figured she would be upset when she got home and found out someone jacked her credit card up to a little over $5400.00. Dallen did the math in his head.

"Lets see, Coach clutch bags 2 at $560.00 a piece, the Louis Vuitton was around $1,200.00 the watch and the 2 sets of diamond studs," Not bad Dallen, he said to himself. The Coach clutches were on sale so he didn't feel bad.

They were multi-color and one was bright, one was pastel. He knew they were different from what the China man had around the way. These were authentic with papers and all; the Sisters would eat those up. The designer bags and earrings would be his get by money for groceries and he needed to put at least $60.00 on his light bill to keep them on.

"I'll make it up to her," Dallen said to himself while he reached the customer service desk were a clerk waited.

"I need a safe until we dock," Dallen told the clerk in a rushed tone.

79

She pushed a form towards him while she turned her back and went through a row of keys. She pulled one from the set and turned back around to Dallen.

"Twenty-five dollar deposit", she handed him the key. Dallen gave her a blank stare, he didn't have any more cash except the $15.00 he knew he needed for cab fare later.

"You can charge it to your room," she said with a country accent.

Relief flooded over Dallen.

"Fine," he said, "Room 210." The clerk punched it in the computer and let him past to the safe.

He quickly locked up his bags except the pretty panty set he got for Vevee.
He rushed back to the free breakfast buffet and filled up two plates with fruit and danish.

Dallen added 2 coffees with cream and sugars on the side and managed to balance all of this on a tray and headed back to the room.

Chapter Nine

9.

<u>Vevee</u>

Vevee was becoming a little nervous. He was taking kind of long to return to the room. What if he wanted her to be gone when he returned?

"But he told me to go to sleep while he went to get something to eat" she thought to herself.

Vevee paced back in forth in the small cabin.

She had put back on her bra and panties and found his bathrobe and put it on. She felt confused.

Just then Dallen pushed the door open and yelled, "Help me out women."

Vevee ran and pulled open the door, Dallen came in with tray full of food and a small pink shopping bag. Vevee let him put the tray down and then stepped right into his arms. He was surprised but welcomed the affection. Vevee gave him a long hug and a kiss on the neck.

She hadn't brushed her teeth yet so she didn't want to kiss him in the mouth. He returned the squeeze and then stepped back to hand her a coffee.

They went over to the small chairs pushed in the corner of the cabin next to a table that shot out of the wall like a little shelve. It was just big enough to set the tray of food on. They nibbled on the breakfast and talked about the rest of the activities that were going on the ship.

There was only one more full day of the cruise left. Dallen lied and told her he was going to try and rest and maybe get a massage before it ended.

Not to be out done, Vevee said she was going for a facial and a massage and maybe check out the R& B bands later in one of the many lounges. She told him one of the singers looked like an old classmate on the flyer that was posted and she wanted to see up close if it was or not.

"I'm just going to rest," Dallen repeated, "Take it easy and enjoy the last leg of this trip. Shoot after you girl, I'm going back to catch some z'ss first, you gave me a work out!"

Dallen smacked her naked thigh playfully as he sipped coffee and splayed his legs out. One he propped up on the bed.

"O.k.," Vevee thought to herself, "that's the second time he said he was tired and wanted to rest. I can take a hint. He didn't offer to join me to see the band but I won't trip. This was nice and let's leave it at that."

Vevee stood up with her coffee and walked over to the bathroom. She took a long sip of her coffee, put it down on the side of the sink and rinsed her face with warm water.

Dallen took this opportunity to place her credit card back in her clutch. Pretending to straighten up a little he moved things around and turned on the music.

Dallen walked up behind her while she was drying her face on one of the many peach color towels in the bathroom. He hugged her around the waist and handed her the pink bag. Vevee smiled and looked surprised.

She saw him enter with the bag but thought he had to grab some toiletries or something personal for himself. She opened the bag and gasped at the beautiful silk bra and panty set.

"OH Dallen," she sincerely exclaimed, "You are so sweet."

"Vevee listen," Dallen started, "When I saw you get off the plane in that yellow halter, I couldn't take my eyes off you. Yellow is your color Baby.

I just wanted to get you something so you
could remember me even if we don't see
each other after this.

I know some women come on this cruise to
relax and escape and I didn't ask you a
whole lot about your relationships, past or
present, but if you are single I would love
for us to keep in touch. But if you are not,
just think of me when you put your sweet
pussycat in those panties girl."

Dallen finished his speech and looked Vevee
straight in the eye. She looked up from the
panty set into his eyes.

"Wow." Vevee thought, "This is different."

"Well Dallen, I am single and would love
for us to stay in touch."

Vevee walked quickly across to the room, grabbed her business card out of her clutch purse and gave it to him. She kissed him and he kissed her back. The morning breath was calmed from fresh fruit and coffee. Before they started again Vevee pulled back and went to put on her dress.

She didn't want to seem so desperate and wanted to leave a little mystery. She dressed slowly sort of waiting for him to offer to meet her later to listen to the band. That didn't happen.

Back in her room Vevee called her friend Mandi.

"Girl, my night was the bomb. Yes, Hell Yes, he was all of that!

The brother even bought me a gift!
WooWee I'm telling you girlfriend, it was
well worth the trip. I got to come Cruisin
more often!"

She chatted with Mandi for over an hour
filling her in on every juicy detail. She also
told her of the mixed signal he gave about
him wanting to keep in touch but rest up and
relax, without her obviously for the
remainder of the cruise.

"Don't trip Ve," Mandi said. "You know
how men can be, maybe you put it on him,
and sometimes that scares them for a
minute. Plus it is only a 3 day cruise. Let
the man chill, ya'll been together pretty
much for a whole day and night!

Do you girlfriend, at least you got some silky draws out of the deal. That's more than that loser ex boyfriend of yours ever got you."

Mandi laughed into the phone and Vevee joined in.

"Your right, I'm going to do me and enjoy the rest of my time."

Vevee hung up the phone and ran a hot bubble bath using some of the special bubble bath she got from the boutique on the ship.

Soon the room smelled like soft flowers and a little peppermint from the candle she burned. Vevee poured herself some champagne and climbed into the tub.

She reminisced on her evening with Dallen for the rest of the morning into the afternoon.

Chapter Ten

10.

Dallen

Dallen thought she would never leave. He
waited until she got in the elevator and hit
the stairs back to the safe deposit box area.
He didn't want anything charged to his
room. He didn't want any hassle of getting
off the ship and he didn't want any
overage's charged to his card. Despite his
shameful hustle, Dallen was trying to turn
his life around. Starting with paying his
credit card debt off.

The same clerk was at the desk. He waved
the key as she looked confused.
"You changed your mind?"

"Yes, you didn't charge it to my room did
you?" Dallen asked.

"No Sir, she answered, "not yet,"
She moved aside so he could go by.

The safe room had around 15-20 safes on
one wall. Dallen pulled the bags out of the
safe and gave the girl the key.

He hit the stairs back to the room where he
packed all his belongings away in case
someone came by.

He went down to the lunch buffet and grabbed as much food as he possibly could and brought it back up to his room. He switched the small TV on and lay back on the bed.

"Yo, Tee, it's me Dallen," Dallen talked into his cell phone,
 "When I get back tomorrow I'm a have some real shit dude."

He switched back into his street slang to talk to his boy from around the way. Teeto owned a small hole in the wall bar, two doors down from where his mom's use to work. That's how Dallen knew Teeto, he use to come into that bar to sell hot stuff and try and talk to his mom's.

Teeto couldn't believe how old she was let alone that she was Dallen's mom.

"Dallen my Man, where you been? What you got?" Teeto always asked one question and then another before you could answer the first.

"Big Jayson and Jeffree are having a party down at the spot Friday night man, if your back by then come by with whatever you have, I have to go man, someone is waiting for me," Teeto ended his call.

"Sweet," Dallen thought, "that is just what I wanted to hear."

Dallen checked the lock on his door and closed his eyes for rest.

Chapter Eleven

11.

Vevee

The rest of the day and evening seemed to fly by for Vevee. She was anxious waiting for her room phone to ring. When that didn't happen, she tried to take advantage of the last social activities.

Vevee ate by the pool hoping to see Dallen. She participated in a scavenger hunt, no Dallen.

She went to see the band, stayed till they started breakin down and chatted with the drummer. He turned out to be an old

classmate, Jay Fresno. That was the familiar face on the poster she saw earlier.
She caught up with him until the early hours. They even took a walk around the ship. Still, no sight of Dallen and no call from Dallen.

Finally she let her old classmate go, and wandered back to her cabin. Vevee felt good about seeing him again and him complimenting her on how beautiful and put together she turned out to be.

Jay teased her about the old days when she wore her hair in a mushroom and always had a watermelon lipsmacker around her neck.

"Bonnie Bell," Vevee laughed as she thought back to the popular brand of lip gloss you just had to have if you were with the "cool" crowd.

Although Jay hadn't changed a lot, she did remind him of the green cut offs he wore on the regular to match his white converse with the green laces.

She remembered him as a sort of geeky tall dude, always carrying an instrument, but always had a geeky girlfriend.

Jay was newly married to a woman from Miami where they just brought a new townhouse. After that story Vevee figured she aught to let him go ahead back to his cabin. He started hinting that the marriage wasn't perfect, and that he could keep her company, no strings, strictly confidential.

Although he had a beautiful complexion, light brown eyes and the longest lashes she had ever seen on a man, Vevee gave him the thanks, but no thanks hug and a kiss on the cheek goodbye.

Back in her room at 2:00 am, Vevee was tempted to call Dallen's room. She washed her face, put on a sexy teddy she bought new for the trip and laid down. She imagined her phone ringing and her getting up to let Dallen in. Her imagination took over while she drifted to sleep, dreaming of his warm embrace.

The next morning Vevee woke fresh and ready to go. She wanted off the ship. Vevee didn't feel like running into Dallen after lusting for him all night. She wanted to take her silky panty set and get home. Once she was home, she could go over the chain of events of the trip and think about calling Dallen. Although she was a little angry, she wanted to see him again and didn't want to wait unit the next vacation.

Her job was picking up and as a sales executive for a major interior design firm, she knew her down time was coming to an end.

"Oh well," Vevee though to herself, "I'll throw myself into my job when I get back, that's always there for me."

Vevee showered and put on a cotton short set. She ordered room service and started packing. She placed all her toiletries on the small table and noticed her cell phone laying there. She pushed the button to make sure she hadn't missed any calls while she was in the shower. To her surprise, the missed call sign flashed on the screen. Vevee quickly pushed o.k. to view. To her disappointment it was a 1-800 number.

Annoyed Vevee threw her phone hard at the pillows on the bed. It bounced around and landed in the middle of the bed. She went over picked up the phone and viewed the number again. Vevee pushed the button that re-dials the missed number and listened to the recording that came on. Her credit card company was calling to verify sales. Vevee appreciated the service that the company offered. Every time she purchased something while she was out of state, they would leave a message to confirm it was actually her. Vevee didn't want to think about the thousand dollars worth of stuff she bought from the ships beautiful and overpriced boutiques so she hung up. She knew the company would automatically call back at least another 2 times until she answered or called back and punched in her numbers and a code that signified everything was o.k. If you didn't agree with the purchases or the amount being charged, you hit 0 and had to speak with a customer service rep. Vevee figured when she got home and settled, she would call and figure out her finances. She grabbed her pocketbook and checked her wallet to make sure she hadn't been pick pocketed during her busy last day.

Her credit card was there so she put her pocketbook aside and continued to pack. Glancing at her cell phone laying there not ringing, she was having a hard time getting Dallen off her mind.

Chapter Twelve

12.

Dallen

Waking from his deep sleep, Dallen felt refreshed. He would make his usual exit off the ship. Last passenger off before the bands, entertainers and crew. He would hang back with the stragglers. The stragglers knew that one passenger's loss was another's gain. Dallen thought back to his last cruise. He hung back with the stragglers, took one last lap around the pool area claiming to try and find his IPOD, and came across an obviously new Izod jacket and matching Izod loafers. The jacket was a little snug but the shoes were just his size. The jacket was an odd shade of green, one Dallen would have never picked for himself.

To "Metro-sexual," Dallen thought to himself. Paired with his linen pants or his light wash jeans, Dallen looked like a dressed down executive. Smiling he thought back to 2 occasions "every time I wear that set, I get pussy or head."

He finished the lap around the pool and came off with 1 pair of gently used Ray Bans.

Chapter Thirteen

13.

Vevee and Dallen

Looking around the baggage claim area,
Vevee couldn't believe she didn't see Dallen
before she got off the ship. Vevee hung near
the shuttle to airport area for an extra half
hour. She caught the second one instead of
the one that was waiting. She had plenty of
time to grab her short flight back to
Connecticut.

Just when the thought of being totally
played by Dallen started to set in, her cell
phone rang. Vevee cleared her throat as she
immediately recognized Dallen's area code
710 showed on the phone.

While Vevee was dining with Dallen on the ship, he left his cell phone on the table while he used the men's room. Just out of curiosity, Vevee looked in the menu of his phone and found his cell phone number. She quickly jotted it down on a piece of paper in her purse. This was before they kicked it and Dallen had not even hinted at keeping in touch after the cruise. Vevee took the number "just in case". She didn't know where the night would end but she loved how it was going. She wanted a chance to make that "just calling to see whats up" call if she got lonely.

"Good Morning," Vevee answered the phone and tried to sound upbeat.

"Hey beautiful, this is Dallen," he paused to give her time to recognize his voice, "how are you making out?"

"Oh Hey Dallen," Vevee tried to sound surprised. "I'm just getting home; I'm actually at the baggage claim. How about you? Are you home?"

Vevee wanted to know more about Dallen and his personal life. He was very stingy with the details when they conversed on the ship. Did someone pick him up from the airport? A women or his boy he mentioned? Was he going home to an empty house like he said or was someone waiting for his fine ass?

"Yeah, I'm home, just got in not to long ago. I was thinking about you and wondering if you made it home safe."

Vevee smiled, someone's actually worried if I got home safe.

"Yes Dallen, thanks for checking on me, my sister is coming to pick me up, she should be outside."

"Vevee, is that a smile I hear in your voice.?" Dallen had game.

Vevee smiled even bigger. She wasn't sure how to answer.

"Yes Dallen, that is a smile. When I didn't see you before we got off the ship, I was disappointed, I wanted to say goodbye to you."

What the hell, Vevee thought, I'm gonna let it all hang out, keep it real. If I scare him off, may as well be early on.

Dallen felt a strange warm feeling creep up his neck into his face. Her voice and her honesty struck Dallen.

"Well," Dallen stuttered trying to regain his composure.

He was expecting a blow off because she hadn't tried to get in touch with him that last day; he thought he was below her standards financially. He didn't have a web page or any proof of success the career type he usually targeted looked for in a future mate. Dallen was use to that reaction. After he didn't invite the women he hustled anywhere or brag about a fancy car or condo, most lost interest.

That worked to his advantage. This time he felt something different.

"I was wondering about you also," Dallen started.

"When you didn't call me that last day, I wanted to give you your space, but really, I wanted to see you and make love to you again." Dallen felt like a huge weight had been lifted.

I'm gonna try something different this time, he thought to himself. He was quiet while he waited for her reaction.

"Ahhhh, Man," Vevee laughed into the phone, "Why are you calling me teasing me Dallen, you want me to get back on this plane?"
Dallen laughed too. They shared a quick conversation and Dallen ended the call by telling Vevee he would check back in with her later when she got settled or tomorrow if it got too late.
Vevee agreed and hung up.

She rushed out of the airport looking for her sister bursting with excitement. She couldn't wait to tell her sister Vindy about her hot new man!

Chapter Fourteen

14.

<u>Dallen</u>

Laying all the items he charged on Vevee's
card across the bed, Dallen made a list. He
use to keep everything in his head but he
was getting older. He remembered the last
time he got the diamond studs, he swore this
woman he was fooling with stole them, but
he couldn't prove it. He questioned how
many pairs he had got because he always
burnt up the receipts.

One pair of diamond studs were going to his
girl Lily who he owed big time.

She helped him when times were tight and when nights were cold and lonely. He texted her and was expecting her to show up later that evening.

He would take the other pair of diamond studs, bags and watches down to Big Jeffree and Jayson's party and unload them the next night. The most expensive watch with the bezels, he would make a few calls tonight and have Lily hang with him to try and meet up with the big ballers. It was always better to have someone with you that you could trust than to hustle alone. He wanted to unload the stuff, the sooner the better.

His apartment didn't have the greatest security and he couldn't afford an alarm system.

Dallen was seriously thinking of making this his last hustle after he went over the profit he would make. Not much more than get by money, but at least his rent would be paid. He promised himself Monday morning he would start on his job search. Rework his resume; use some of the money he was going to make on getting a haircut and a new work suit. Not the casual stuff he bought on the cruise.

He hadn't called Vevee like he promised but he didn't want to seem like he was rushed to get at her. Dallen was a man with pride and an ego. Even though he was feeling her, he would make her wait.

Parts of his feelings were tied to all the stuff he jacked from her card. He wanted to get rid of and forget about it.

In the back of his mind he thought about getting caught like he usually did with the merchandise sitting in his cramped closet in his cramped apartment. That thought usually stayed with him until a few weeks after he unloaded everything.
He would call Vevee when he was ready to maybe talk about meeting up with her again, and not until then.

Chapter Fifteen

15.

<u>Vevee</u>

Vevee paced as she spoke with the Visa card representative on the phone. She finally got around to returning the banks call, she was blown away. Her temperature rose as she listened to the women on the other end. Her card had been jacked up to the tune of five-thousand dollars and some change. The bank would cover it all except the one-thousand and change she admitted to, but let her know they would be initiating and investigation and prosecuting to the fullest extent. The representative went on to mention if she knew anything or even had an idea who or what happened, she better come clean now.

Vevee took deep breaths and sat down. She was insulted by the women insinuating that she would charge up expensive men's watches and 2 and 3 designer bags, 2 identical pair of diamond stud earrings then not own up to it. She let the women have a taste of her frustration.

"For your information Miss, I work very hard every day and own a few designer bags and nice and expensive things. But I worked for them and paid for them. As you can see from my account I am a responsible spender. I do not have the time to play games to profit a few thousand dollars worth of crap. Please don't insult me I am surly not in the mood."

The women calmed her down by repeating
the phrases Vevee was sure she used on all
the pissed off customers. She told Vevee
she would be surprised how many people
claim theft, and then the investigation
unfolds only to reveal pictures of the
customer wearing the items claimed in plain
sight.

"No offense Ms. Taylor, I'm supposed to
give this information to everyone who has
credit card theft and possible stolen
identity."

The representative explained the paperwork
would be coming Federal Express and hung
up.

Vevee sat in her comfy green loveseat and
hugged the pillow.

"Why can't life be easy for a while? now I gotta go through this."

Vevee sat for a half hour and went over her days on the cruise. A sinking feeling started to build in her stomach. She thought of Dallen and the fact that he had not called. She went to her bedroom and picked up the wrinkled itinerary from the cruise off of her vanity. She walked back into her kitchen and put the kettle on for tea.

Her plan was to go over her days on the ship step by step to see who could be a suspect. She flashed back to waking up in Dallen's cabin, taking in the wonderful view of him in shorts with no shirt on. Looking fine as ever.

A sinking feeling started in her stomach as she wondered how long he had been awake. She pushed that to the back of her mind. The credit card representative had told her to make a list.

"Think of anyone you spent time with on the cruise who you left with access to your bag."

Vevee didn't want to make a list. She sat back at her kitchen table with her tea. She wanted to forget the whole ordeal. Sitting looking around her small apartment she spied her bible on the small bookcase she had over in the computer area. Vevee didn't go to church on the regular, like her mother wished she would, but she read her bible at least once a week. Her book mark had a tiny gold angel dangling on one end.

She opened to

Acts 14:22 We must go through many
hardships to enter the kingdom of God.

Vevee had used the bible and this particular
scripture to get over her last breakup.
She realized she wasn't perfect in the Lords
eyes and was still a work in progress. Vevee
had a strong faith that helped her through
many a trial growing up.

"What am I doing wrong God?" Vevee
prayed, "How many more hardships?" She
thought about all the things she had been
doing that would not have been pleasing to
God.

Vevee recalled the guilty feeling that came
over her at one point on the cruise.

Her and Dallen were at dinner and he left to go the men's room. She remembered making the decision to sleep with him based on the fact that the blonde woman that was hitting on him on his stroll to the men's room, would most likely sleep with him if she didn't. A decision based on not what was in her heart but what she felt between her thighs.

The champagne was also a factor in her decision. Not accustomed to one night stands, she had figured one in her lifetime couldn't hurt.

"Now look," Vevee thought to herself, "I done gave it up to a man who may have stolen from me. Ewwww, creepy."

Why would Dallen steal from her? She sat and pondered. He didn't look poor.

She recalled the soft material of his pant suit and the sexy smelling subtle cologne he wore and his diamond stud in one ear, she swore it was real. She thought of the pretty yellow panty sent he bought her. Although it wasn't a high end designer name on it, not one thing in the cruise ships boutiques was what you would call cheap.

He wouldn't buy her something and then steal from her Or would he? Vevee's head felt heavy and she leaned back on the chair cushions.

She thought about her choice of men and thought back to her last relationship. She thought of how she had tried to pull herself closer to God to help save it. But that relationship was not to be saved. While sitting in church with her sister

Vindy, she realized she was in the relationship for all the wrong reasons. What she craved couldn't be fulfilled by any man. Only God could make her feel complete.

Her ex-man wasn't the worst, but he certainly wasn't what she always hoped for.

The relationship lacked any fire or passion. Her ex was dependable which was a big plus. He was always there, but would never go above or beyond to please her.

He never took interest in anything she was interested in. He gave her the impression that if she could pick up the house they rented, all the belongings she bought to furnish it and physically move herself and everything at once, he would still be sitting in the same spot.

Maybe he would get up and leave long enough to visit a bar and pick up the next women who could cook, clean, keep house and freely give him sex, offer up ½ the rent and go to family functions once in a while, he would go sit back down in the same spot and be perfectly content. He would always say "Look Babe, I'm doing the best I can here."

That sounded so lame at 4:30 in the morning, the usual time he would return home after a Friday or Saturday night of drinking with the guys. During the week he would hang around the house, watching sports or playing videos. Once in a while he would suggest they go out, but not often. If he worked overtime, he would make an effort which was about once a year.

Vevee returned to reading her bible.

Why after getting rid of her ex, going to bible study 3 Wednesdays in a row, and giving up smoking, she was still having drama?

"Why God? She spoke softly out loud. "What is it you want me to do now?"

She thought of how she jumped into bed with Dallen who was a perfect stranger to her before they hooked up.

"Well, yeah, that probably wasn't the smartest thing, but I thought I felt a connection." Vevee put her head in her hand and closed her eyes.
Thinking back to the cruise and the fun she was having on it, she reminisced about her and Dallen dancing and drinking and leaning into each other on the dance floor.

She opened her eyes and thumbed through her bible some more. She turned to *Samuel 16:7 The Lord does not look at the things man looks at. Man looks at the outward appearance, but the Lord looks at the heart.*

Vevee remembered picking Dallen out of the crowd on straight looks. She didn't really care what his conversation was like.

"Maybe I should have taken my time to check out his heart, oh well," she thought as she continued to flip through her Bible.

She came across *Psalm 32:10 Many are the woes of the wicked, but the Lord's unfailing love surrounds the man who trusts him.* Lastly she turned to *Proverbs 4:25 Let your eyes look straight ahead, fix your gaze directly before you.*

With that, Vevee shut her Bible and got up. She placed it on the ottoman in front of her and threw her pillow on the floor. She paced around the small living space.

"OK God, I am going to fix my gaze in front of me, I am going to get through this with your help, and I am going to keep it moving." She felt sadness lift off her chest.

Vevee walked into the kitchenette and fixed another cup of tea. She grabbed her pen and pad and sat down at the table. She thought out loud to herself.

"I am going to make my list and mail this stuff back to the credit card company so I can put this behind me. If Dallen calls, I am going to tell him what happened and see what his reaction is, maybe then I can tell if it was him or not.

If he doesn't call, I will forget about it and be more careful next time."

She recalled her favorite passage and said it outloud.

"When times are good, be happy; but when times are bad, consider: God has made the one, as well as the other." *Ecclesiastes 7:14*

Vevee started working on her list of possible suspects.

Chapter Sixteen

16.

Dallen

A few months had passed since the cruise
and Dallen was feeling good. He had landed
a bartending gig with a catering company
working straight through the summer at
weddings, corporate functions and wild
parties. Lily had connected him with the DJ
and he was in after the DJ introduced him to
the owner of the catering company.

Lily had appreciated the pair of diamond
stud earrings he bought her from the cruise.
That put Dallen back in her good graces.

While he was dating around and they understood they were not committed to each other, they slept together on the regular and Dallen was starting to slow down in his pursuit of women. He thought Lily had something to do with that and it scared him a little.

He was able to unload all the goods he got off of Vevee's credit card except the last pair of diamond studs. The watch went first and he got the full $1,500.00 he had wanted. He thought briefly of contacting Vevee.

She was fun, kinda cute. He considered calling her a time or two, but dismissed the idea when he thought of bringing her out in his old car, then taking her back to his tight apartment. The fact that she had not contacted Dallen was a good sign to him.

Usually his victim would call upset after they heard from the credit card company, some would even straight out accuse him. He finessed it off every time.

Women's ego's, especially the high powered executive type, were as big as and sometimes bigger than any mans. This allowed him to run game and have the women remembering their night of hot passion and forgetting that he had access to their credit cards. Since the amounts that he stole were small potatoes to most of the women, they just wanted to be reassured they had not been played by a man they gave it up to. Most were too embarrassed to really pursue it any longer than the couple of weeks it took for the credit card company to close the case. Maybe Vevee had someone and wasn't thinking about me or the crap that was charged to her card.

Just then his cell phone rang; it was his boss from the catering company. He asked Dallen if he wanted to bring someone on the next gig.

It was a party on a small yacht and they were both allowed one guest. The guy giving the party wanted to have a certain amount of people at the function; he didn't care if he didn't know them. Some people were funny; he went on to say, all about appearances. He told Dallen to think about it and call him in the evening. If he didn't want to bring someone, he would use his slot and bring his sister along with his wife. Dallen thanked him and told him he would probably bring someone and would call him back to confirm. When he hung up he immediately thought of Lily.

She was so beautiful and exotic looking, he sometimes didn't want her around.

He smiled while he thought of the verse from the Jackson 5 song I Want You Back. That verse talked about him not wanting her around cuz pretty faces always seem to stand out in the crowd. Lily always attracted extra attention.

With the recent death of the King of Pop Michael Jackson, Dallen heard all the songs he loved growing up on the radio and television. This was a wakeup call for Dallen. He began to think about his lifestyle and the fact that he didn't have any kids yet. He wanted at least one child before his number was called.

While Lily was an exotic beauty and would definitely produce a beautiful child, she never even mentioned children. Their relationship was based on a quiet, easy understanding to take each other as they were flaws and all and not to question too much.

Dallen never even asked Lily is she ever had kids or if she planned on having any. Dallen knew deep down that the relationship was based more on necessity than love. He longed for a fresh start with a new girlfriend who he could grow with and raise a child with. He pictured him and his new girlfriend and brand new baby boy rolling into church on Sunday.

He pictured Vevee, the women from the cruise in a soft green flowing dress.

He reminisced about him and Vevee and the time they spent on the cruise. How impressed she would be with a fancy party on a yacht. He didn't have to bring her back to his apartment; he could get a room near the area where the boats docked. There was a Courtyard by Marriott in the area. He decided to make that call. He walked to his bedroom and dug out her number from his bedside table. He had a drawer full of business cards. The pile had grown since he started his bartending job. He picked up the card with the dark purple ink on the mint green, expensive stock business card that read

Vevee Taylor. He dialed the number and waited for her to pick up.

"Hello Vevee? This is me Dallen Page, from the cruise a few months ago," he paused, and heard Vevee suck her breath.

"Oh hey Dallen", Vevee tried to compose herself.

The call had caught her totally off guard. After completing her list of suspects from the cruise fiasco, she had realized she had also left her old classmate whom she hung out with one night on the cruise, with access to her bag.

The credit card representative told her that sometimes it was an inside job at the boutique. She had chalked it up to a loss and decided to move on. She thought about

Dallen the other day when she pulled out the panty set that he had bought her. Vevee had spoken with her girlfriend about the whole situation and her girl had assured her not to beat herself up to much.

"Vevee, Mandi exclaimed into the phone, "Don't worry girl, God is watching you and what goes around, will surly come back around. You know God don't like ugly."

Mandi had recently joined the church and peppered her comments with God this and Jesus that. This did make Vevee feel a little better, that whoever stole from her, would eventually get theirs.

Now, holding her cell phone in her hand while looking for her car in the mall parking lot, Vevee had mixed feelings.

"What's up with you Dallen? I hadn't heard from you in a minute so I thought you forgot about me."

"Naww Sis," Dallen replied, "I been busy working. I'm trying to have you come out here and see me. I have a gig on a yacht I thought you might enjoy." He put it out there plain and waited for her reply.

His voice sounded good to Vevee. She remembered the hot sex they had. She also remembered the last date she had been on with a lame, tiered dude and the fact that she had not had sex since the cruise. Her body longed for Dallen's touch.

"Well Dallen, if you e-mail me the information, I will look at my calendar and call you back. Do you have access to a computer and an e-mail address?"

"Yes," Dallen was relieved that he had recently invested in a laptop computer to try and come up to speed with the rest of the world.

He was paying a monthly internet bill bundled with his cell and cable. He wrote down her e-mail information and told her he was looking forward to seeing her again.

When they hung up, Dallen felt a little annoyed. Women hardly ever turned him down or waited to check a schedule before telling him yes. He shot off a quick e-mail detailing the time, date and location of the party. Where he could pick her up or meet her, and even included the hotel information to try and appear Gentleman like. He paced around his apartment.

His eye spied the blue and green bag with the last pair of diamond stud earrings from the cruise.

"If she acts right" Dallen thought, "I'll use some of the money I'll make from selling those on her."

Dallen walked over to the bag and took out the white earring box. He shoved the box deep in his pants pocket and placed the blue and green plastic bag on his dresser. Just then the "ding" sounded telling him he had new e-mail. Dallen sat down and looked at the return message from Vevee. It read: "Looks like a good date and time for me, I will meet you at the Courtyard Suites. :D."

Dallen liked the smiley face at the end of the sentence.

He sent back: "See you then."

And signed off. Dallen headed out the door to make some cash, at least five hundred dollars was what he hoped for.

Chapter Seventeen

17.

Vevee

Vevee decided this would be a great opportunity to talk to Dallen in person. That way she could see his reaction when she told him about the credit card deal. She would judge him then. If he did turn up guilty, she could go back to the hotel, get a massage and call it a weekend getaway. Time would tell. Vevee felt excited about seeing him again.

Dallen

When it was time to meet Vevee at the hotel, Dallen had everything ready. He had a new outfit. His white shirt that was mandatory for his gig on the Yacht was straight out of the cleaners fresh and starched. He was going to have champagne and chocolate covered strawberry's delivered to his room at 11:00 pm. This way, when he got her back to the room, he could further impress her with his thoughtfulness. Dallen was really trying this time. Considering the short time they had on the cruise together, he wasn't sure if she was the one for him, but she was well worth a try.

He really started to feel the urge to produce an offspring.

From what he could tell about Vevee, she
was smart and employed with no mental or
physical defects which were a damn good
start as far as Dallen was concerned.
He unpacked some of his toiletries and put
them in the bathroom. He had his condoms
in the small plastic blue and green bag from
the jewelry store on the cruise. He placed
the bag on the bedside table.

Dallen showered and changed and went
downstairs to meet Vevee in the lounge like
they agreed.

Chapter Eighteen

18.

Vevee and Dallen

The party on the yacht was more than Dallen
could have hoped for. The crowd was a
good mix of younger and older, rich and not
so rich and even a few politicians thrown in
with a local celebrity or two.

He watched Vevee from his station at the
bar. She seemed to enjoy herself and mingle
easily, conversing with the women as well
as the men. One man hung around her and
must have propositioned her.

Vevee pointed over to the bar and laughed as the man handed her a business card but moved on to the next. After that, a bar stool freed up at the bar and Vevee came and sat there for the rest of the night. They laughed and talked easily about the party and different places they both had been and seen.

Vevee didn't want to bring up the credit card issue. It didn't seem like the right time or place. She did wonder what happened to his construction job. Dallen had not mentioned he was a bartender at all that weekend on the cruise. Oh well, she figured, at least he is working.

Judging from the tip jar, that was as big as a gallon of milk and filled to the top, he wasn't doing that badly.

They got back to the hotel around 2:00ish. Vevee excused herself to her room to leave her personal belongings. If Dallen was a thief, he wouldn't get her again. She noticed the disappointment in his voice when she told him she would stop in her room first before heading to his.

"Don't take to long, Vee, I have a surprise for you."

"O.K Dallen, give me a minute and I'll be right over."

Vevee dropped her bag and shoes in her room. She slipped into her flip flops. She used the bathroom and checked herself in the mirror. Vevee left on her fabulous dress that was getting her so much attention that night, but welcomed the chance to slip out of the shoes that were killing her feet. She grabbed her key card and headed back down the hall to Dallen's room.

Dallen opened the door on the first knock and pulled her into the room by her waist. They let the door close behind them and shared a deep passionate kiss.

"Oh", Dallen exclaimed, "Your much shorter without your heels, were your dogs barking?" Dallen laughed.

"Beauty is pain," Vevee laughed back and sat on the bed.

Dallen walked over to the table in the corner and took the top off of the silver tray which revealed the chocolate covered strawberries.

"Ohhh, Vevee exclaimed, "My favorite!"

He walked over to the table and poured two glasses of champagne into the glasses that were set out.

"Go Dallen, I'm impressed," she smiled at him.

"Well that's what I was going for," Dallen smiled back.

He had taken off his shoes and had bare feet; his white shirt unbuttoned revealing a white wife-beater tight on his smooth, brown skin. His chest muscles bulged through. He wore an expensive looking chain she hadn't seen because it was long and hidden by his starched button up shirt he wore behind the bar.

In a bold move, Vevee walked over to him and took the chain in her hand. On the end of the chain that was hidden in the top of his wife-beater, two diamond studded initials hung DJ. She looked up confused at him.

"DJ? I thought your last name was Page?" Vevee questioned him.

Dallen didn't stutter or flinch,

"I'm a Junior," he lied right in her eyes. "Dallen Jr."

"Oh," Vevee said and sat back on the bed.

Dallen joined her on the bed. After another glass of champagne and another few strawberries, they both relaxed and started with some heavy foreplay. Dallen's hands and tongue were all over her. She pulled her dress off and undid his pants.

Dallen picked her up and sat her on the chair in the corner. He removed her panties and propped one leg on the maroon colored upholstered arm of the chair and the other leg on the other arm.

Vevee giggled while she let him mold her body however he chose. When he reached for his condoms in the blue and green bag on the night stand, the color of the bag caught Vevee's eye.

Dallen kissed her and rubbed and kissed her titties, then he inserted his fingers into her. Vevee felt herself respond and get super wet and moaned as her temperature rose to hot. He entered her strong and a little rough, when she didn't resist he continued on. Vevee wrapped her arms around his neck and breathed in his sexy smell. She kissed him and sucked his neck.

He held her back with one arm pulling her lower body into him, with the other hand he rubbed her titties causing her to come up off the chair and grind her hips into his hard manhood. They worked each other into a hot, sweaty climax. After they moved to the bed spent and wore out. Dallen and Vevee slept for a while then woke up and made slow easy love again. After, they both fell into a deep sleep.

Chapter Nineteen

19.

<u>Vevee</u>

The sound of the shower woke Vevee out of her sleep. She sat up and swung her legs over the side of the bed. Stepping out of the bed and onto the carpet she wanted to grab her clothes and get down the hall to her own room. Her foot slipped on the blue and green plastic bag that she had seen earlier. Dallen had his condoms in it.

Vevee picked it up and saw that one was left in the bag.

She read the name in cursive navy blue writing: Seaview Jewelers. She had the same bag at home that she got from the cruise. Vevee sat on the bed. She stood up and picked up Dallen's pants off the floor and pulled out his wallet. Vevee quickly pulled out his license. Dallen Jackson it read, she checked the birth date. Her eye zeroed in on the year 66, making Dallen 45 instead of 39 like he told her. Vevee put it back and sat back down on the bed. A sick feeling washed over her.

The shower shut off. She quickly put on her clothes and her flip flops. Vevee felt scared.

She didn't understand why he lied about his name, but the fact that he lied about his age gave Vevee the straight creeps.

"What type of man does that?" she thought to herself.

Dallen came out of the bathroom with a towel wrapped around his waist. Vevee looked startled.

"Good Morning Beautiful" he smiled at Vevee.

"Good Morning," she forced a smile at his line that sounded corny to her.

Vevee got up and walked over to the table picking up her key card.

"You leaving so soon?" Dallen asked.

"Yeah," Vevee replied, "Dallen I had so much fun but I really have to get back. I didn't have no business coming down here with my busy schedule. I have an early morning meeting I need to prepare for so I need to shower and hit the road."

Vevee spoke fast and was at the door before Dallen could stop her.

"O.K. Baby," Dallen replied walking towards her. He kissed her on the cheek and held the door open for her.

"Call me when you get home o.k. I had a good time with you and I'm glad you came to meet me."
Dallen let her walk past him out the door. Vevee looked over her shoulder while she headed down the hall to her room.

"I'll call you as soon as I get home Dallen. Thanks for everything."

Once in her room Vevee kicked off her flip flops and locked the door.

Chapter Twenty

20.

Dallen

Dallen thought Vevee's fast departure was a little strange, but he welcomed it all the same. Now he didn't have to ask about what she wanted for breakfast and try and make small talk until it was time for them to leave.

He walked over to the plastic bag on the floor and picked it up. One condom was left in the bag. Dallen pulled back the covers and found the used rubber under the covers. He picked it up and examined it while he walked in the bathroom to flush it.

He was glad to see no semen was left in the condom which meant his plan worked.

Dallen had cut a small hole in the top of the condom. He planned to knock up Ms. Vevee whether she planned for it or not. He figured if she did become pregnant it was meant to be. He didn't tamper with the first condom he used and figured he would give his wild plan a 50 50 chance. He considered she may not keep the child without his ever knowing about it. He knew most career women did plan out their pregnancies and anything unexpected would have to wait until their career reached a certain stage.

At least that is what happened in Dallen's last relationship. He was still bitter.

Dallen flushed the condom and went to look for the one he left by the chair.

"But if she decides to keep it, Dallen smiled at the thought, "I will have a new little girl or boy. Even if it's only part time parenting."

Dallen had made the decision to keep the baby if Vevee did turn up pregnant and wanted nothing to do with it. He did think of the possibility that she wouldn't think it was his. If she slept around or slept with the next man without protection she wouldn't think of him as the child's father. As far as she knew, they used protection each time.

As an intelligent woman, Dallen reasoned, she knew condoms were not 100 % guaranteed protection. However it played out, Dallen felt better knowing he had a chance of being a parent.

"I gave it my best shot," Dallen said to himself while he lay back in the bed.

Chapter Twenty-One

21.

<u>Vevee</u>

On the road, Vevee talked into her cell phone head piece.

"Yes Mam, I had my account closed because of illegal activity on my card," she explained to the credit card representative on the phone.

"Now I would like to report who I think used my card, I have a name a possible alias and a cell phone number. I want him prosecuted to the fullest."

The Customer service rep placed her on hold and bought up her account.

"This investigation had been closed out months ago. Did you see any of the items that were charged?"

"No," Vevee rushed on "But I saw the bag from the jewelry store on the cruise ship where the items were charged in his possession!"

"And that is where you met this man, right, on the cruise? He may have shopped at that boutique also. Mamm, we would need more proof than that to reopen an account case that has already been settled."
The representative's voice turned flat.
Vevee talked fast,
 "I checked his license and he lied to me about his name and age," she couldn't understand why the representative didn't think this was as big of a deal as she did.

"Don't you people want to catch him and make him pay? That's what you were threatening to do is prosecute to the fullest!"

Vevee's anger and confusion welled up inside her. A tear slid down her cheek. I can't believe this woman has me crying over this shit, Vevee wiped the tear off her cheek while she continued to drive.

She pulled onto a route off the highway and set the cruise control. She figured she would take the less congested road to her apartment.

"Hello, are you still there?" Vevee adjusted her earpiece wondering if the rep had hung up.

"Yes Ms. Taylor, I'm still here, I was just recording all this in your file. I'm going to take the name and information you have. Investigations will decide if this is enough to open the file. If so, they may research the cruise ship records and see if we can match anything up. Maybe we can get an image from the boutique's camera.

Ms. Taylor, you would have to make a positive ID of this man and that may mean travel on your part."

"Whatever it takes," Vevee felt relieved she was finally getting through to the rep.

What a creep, Vevee thought to herself. Flashes of the hot sex they just had popped in her mind. She tried to erase the thoughts and the warm feeling that spread over her.

The rep's voice snapped her out of her daydream.

"Unfortunately Mamm, you may have just met a liar and not a thief. Lots of the men that go on the single cruises are married. They have bonus points built up on the company card so they tell the wife they are going on a business trip and show up on the weekend singles cruise."

Vevee's stomach lurched.

"Married? I never really thought of that," Vevee knew she sounded very naive to the customer service rep.

The representative took down the limited information Vevee had. Since she checked Dallen's license, she had the name, Dallen Jackson, and the town but she was not 100% sure of the street name.

The representative said someone would contact her if the case was reopened.

Vevee thought about Dallen and if he seemed married or not.

He was mysterious and he didn't say much about his home life, or love life, past or present. But he bought me to a public party where none of his co-workers gave a funny vibe and no smart remarks from the other women. Vevee thought to herself. She found herself making excuses for Dallen. Not wanting to admit to herself that he very well may be married. He already had lied to her about his name and age.

Even after he had lied to her she hated to admit she was still feeling him. He had put it on her.

"Well" Vevee thought out loud, "That feeling will wear off and I will move on and take it as a lessoned learned."

Chapter Twenty-Two

22.

Vevee -- Three Months Later

Vevee's period still had not showed up.
After her last visit with Dallen, some three
months ago, she had some spotting so she
counted that as a light period.

The next month things were so busy at work
she barely realized that the time had come
and gone when she was supposed to have
her period. She didn't worry. The only man
she had been with was Dallen and they had
used protection.

She chalked it up to the stress of the whole Dallen fiasco and continued to work 45 to 55 hour work weeks. Another month passed.

This month however, she couldn't ignore the swell and tenderness of her breasts. The nauseous feeling she had in the morning when she tried to scramble eggs. Or the flip floppy feeling in her stomach and the sudden fatigue. Vevee made a doctors appointment.

Vevee sat in her favorite love seat and hugged her pillow. She grabbed the soft, flannel bright yellow pillow and propped it under her head.

Turning long ways and hanging both legs over the opposite end of the love seat, Vevee began to cry.

She didn't know who to tell she was pregnant. She had not told her friend Mandi of her last visit with Dallen. She didn't want her all up in her business.

Vevee knew it wasn't the smartest thing. She didn't want to explain to Mandi her decision to see Dallen again. She couldn't explain it to her mother. She imagined the conversation.

"Yeah Ma, Dallen may have been a con artist that I met on a cruise ship.
We kicked it, caught sexual feelings, met him again, confirmed that he may be the thief that stole from me, even called it in to the credit card company, now, he is most possibly my baby's Daddy."

Vevee thought about being a Mom. The thought appealed to her.

She had saved enough to purchase a condo with all her overtime. She was getting up there in age, and although she had lots of propositions, no man had ever made her feel like being their baby's momma or wife for that matter.

She thought about Dallen. The credit card company never contacted her so she had tried to move forward.

Maybe Dallen was just some married man. He never tried to contact her after their last meeting. She was glad. She didn't want to get mixed up if he was married. There was a strong pull between them that she felt. If she let it continue she would definitely be hooked.

Vevee thought to herself, she would not tell a soul until she contacted Dallen.

She wanted to see if she was going to be a single mom or if there were a possibility that her baby's dad would be in her child's life. Vevee was always one for scoping out the big picture. The long term scenario, it was what made her one of the top paid executives at her job. Because of this, she wouldn't need Dallen for financial support, but she wanted her child to have a sense of their history. She thought it was most important to have a mother and father in the baby's life.

Vevee got out her laptop. Although she had not contacted Dallen since their last meeting, she knew his name was saved in her contacts. Vevee planned to set up a meeting in public, like at a coffee joint or restaurant and tell Dallen then.

If he is married this will be his chance to come clean. She was anxious to find out what his reaction would be.

He may try and pay me off to get rid of it if he is married, or he may want to be a man and agree on visits and shared support, or her favorite scenario, he may want to marry me and move me into his house and take care of me and his child. Maybe this whole lying about his name and age thing was just pure vanity on Dallen's part. I mean I am a fine young sister, maybe he felt to old for me.

Vevee thought to herself "There I go making excuses for him."

Vevee put the laptop back down. She had to think about how to word her e-mail to sound casual.

She let her mind wander as she made herself comfortable on the couch and fell asleep.

When she woke up, Vevee felt refreshed and typed a short e-mail to Dallen and waited for his reply.

Chapter Twenty-Three

23.

Vevee

Vevee's stomach had butterflies as she headed to the restaurant to meet Dallen. She was early, she wanted to be seated when he walked in. Before she reached her car, her cell phone rang. It was the detective for the credit card company. The detective went on to explain to Vevee that they had a lead on the suspect accused of fraud and they were going to bring him in soon and she would have to come identify him.

Vevee felt confused and sick to her stomach. She explained that she was actually on her way to meet Dallen.

"Is it Dallen Page you are bringing in for fraud charges? I mean Dallen Jackson?" Vevee questioned the detective; she wanted to be sure they were talking about the same person. She wasn't really sure what last name he was using.

Vevee was hoping and praying that the thief turned out to be someone else. Since she became pregnant she was hoping for the best possible scenario. That meant having Dallen in their baby's life.

"Well Mam, it shows several aliases he uses, but yes, Dallen Page is one of them," the detective said.

The detective asked the name of the restaurant and told Vevee he would have the officer wait until she was well out of the way before approaching Dallen.

Dallen

Dallen checked his reflection in the glass of the restaurant as he rounded the corner. His Ray Bans and white shirt with his expensive linen slacks caught the eye of a woman who smiled at him while he reached the entrance. She was exciting while he was coming in.

Dallen had grown use to the attention.

Over the last couple of months, he had done exceptionally well at his job. He had moved up from bartender to part owner in a small sports bar with one of his colleagues.

The original partner wanted out and Dallen happened to be in the right place at the right time and had saved his money.

He had low rent and only a few other bills. He ate for free and partied for free.

The sports bar had been used in a hip-hop video right after he signed on as partner and he and his colleague were enjoying the profits from that. The remodeling that Dallen helped with had paid off in triple. His new upgraded wardrobe and upgraded self confidence oozed from him. Money could change a man.

He was surprised by Vevee's e-mail. She was inviting him to an early dinner next time he was in Connecticut. She mentioned she knew he was there on business from time to time and would wait for his reply.

He couldn't really remember what he had told Vevee about his business. He knew he had stuck to his construction work story on the cruise, but didn't recall talking about it at their last meeting.

Oh well, he thought, it wasn't that important if she wanted to see him again.
He could use the trip to Connecticut to go into New York like him and his partner had been talking about. Certain items for the bar were easy to get and cheaper in New York.

He thought about her and his crazy pregnancy scheme. If it actually worked, he would be happy. Dallen would demand a paternity test. He was not trying to raise anyone else's child, at least not under false pretense.

They talked through e-mail and Vevee
invited him to an early dinner at a restaurant
not far from her home.

As he opened the door to the restaurant he
saw Vevee sitting in the corner booth. She
looked better than he remembered.
Her pretty eyes and smooth complexion
stood out against the dull brown of the vinyl
booth. She smiled as she saw him walk in.

Vevee

Dallen looked more handsome than Vevee
remembered. She wanted to let him know
she was pregnant, but was hoping they could
spend time together and that he would be a
part of their baby's life.

Now, when he walked in the restaurant
Vevee was rethinking her decision but she
knew it was too late.

She saw the police car parked in the shade when she entered the restaurant.

"Hi Vevee," Dallen leaned in and gave her a kiss on the cheek.

"Hi Dallen," Vevee gave him a hug. She couldn't help but smile despite her mixed emotions.

"Maybe I'll warn him," Vevee thought to herself. "That way he won't be surprised when the police approach him and he can at least have time to call an attorney before the police take him down to the station."

"Why am I trying to help this man who stole from me?" Vevee was trying to clear her head but was having flashbacks of their passionate love making.

The waitress came over and Dallen ordered an ice tea and a burger.

Vevee pretended to check her phone while her mind raced.

Vevee and Dallen

Dallen ate his food while Vevee did most of the talking.

For 30 minutes Vevee talked. She stayed focused on her pregnancy and not the pending fraud charges. While talking about it and her mixed feelings, Vevee became teary eyed. Just dealing with the topic of becoming a Mom out of wedlock overwhelmed Vevee.

"So that's when I got a pregnancy test done." VeVee fished out the results from her pocketbook. She handed Dallen the official looking paper that had her diagnosis on it.

Between 14 and 16 weeks pregnant the document stated. She also showed him her prescription for pre-natal vitamins.

"Vevee, I hope you don't take offense when I ask for a paternity test. It's just that it would have been when you came down to the party on the yacht and we kicked it. If you do the math, that was about 4 months ago. But, we used protection remember. Both times. Also, you were acting a little funny that night, in a rush to leave. I thought you were trying to get back to your man here in Connecticut."

Dallen looked at Vevee and saw her eyes watering. He had to play the role and hide his excitement about what he considered good news.

"Vevee don't cry, I'm not saying you're making this up, I'm just saying. You're a fine successful woman. It's hard to believe you don't have someone who would be waiting to be your baby's father."

Dallen finished and put his hand on top of Vevee's.

Vevee let the tears flow. She let Dallen rest his hand on top of hers. It comforted her. She used the other hand to dab her eyes with tissue.

"What a mess," she thought to herself.

"Well Dallen, there is something else I need to tell you." Vevee took a big sip of her ice water. She knew the police weren't going to wait forever so she figured she may as well get it over with.

"Dallen you are going to be approached by the officer in the parking lot when you leave here. They called me about fraud charges they have on you. It just so happened that my credit card was stolen on the cruise we went on and they think it was you."

Vevee left out the part about her calling the representative after their last visit. It didn't make a difference who initiated the investigation as far as Vevee was concerned. She wanted to know who she was dealing with. Was he just a fine ass black man with great sex? Or a shady con man with a lot of different names and address and secrets.

Dallen looked shocked. He stared at Vevee with his mouth open. He took a sip of his ice tea and got up from the booth.

Vevee watched.

"Is he going to run outside?" She said to herself.

Dallen walked near the window, glanced outside at the cop car under the tree in the corner of the lot. He came back to the booth and sat back down.

Vevee started,

"Dallen, I didn't want to believe it was you, you certainly don't look like someone who needs to steal, but you never know now a days. Dallen, did you steal from me?"

Vevee didn't know what to say next so she was quiet waiting for his reply.

Dallen put his elbows on the table and rested his head in both his hands.

"Vevee," Dallen started. He took a deep breath and sat back against the booth.

"Yes, Vevee, I did steal from you on the cruise. Please let me explain."

Vevee sucked her teeth and started to gather her pocketbook and car keys.

Dallen had noticed her Mercedes Benz keys on the table when he first joined her. Now with them in her hand and her looking towards the door he started talking fast.

"I was in a situation and I was up against the wall. When I boarded the ship I got a call from my Mom and she was in a panic. I owed my her some money and I had to come up with it a lot sooner then we agreed upon due to an emergency with her housing. Her and her landlord had a big falling out and she needed the money right away. Vevee, I was in between jobs at that time."

Dallen stared at Vevee to see if she was buying it.

Vevee wanted to believe him so badly. She kept quiet and kept listening.

Dallen continued on.

"When you came to meet me for the party on the yacht, I had plans for us to hang out the next day for dinner and sight-seeing. I had arranged a tour and even planned to take you shopping. Vevee, you and the fact that I stole from you was all I could think about. I was going to try my best to make it up to you. When you came and left so suddenly, I didn't get a chance."

Vevee sat staring at him. She wasn't sure what to believe.

"Vevee, excuse me please while I make a call to my business partner so I can get the name of an attorney to meet me down at the station."

Dallen dialed his cell phone and talked rather loudly into it. Vevee could tell he was nervous.

"Bruce man, it's Dallen. Yeah listen, I got jammed up here in Connecticut on an old warrant I have to take care of. No, I never lived in Connecticut but Bruce man listen, I need the name of an attorney to meet me down at the station, they're gonna take me in."

Vevee sat still and listened.

"Yeah, I got the money for the trip to New York, I can use some of that cash to bond out and I may still be able to pick up a few things for the bar before I head back. Yeah man, don't worry about me, I'll be back."

Dallen stood up and went into his pants pocket. He pulled out a money clip and a stack of cash in a rubber band.

"Vevee," Dallen pushed the money clip towards her across the table, "take this cash and meet me down at the station when I call you. I'm gonna need a ride back down here to my rental car when I bond out. I don't want to bring all this cash down to the station."

"Dallen, Vevee interrupted him, "I don't know..I'm tryin to get my head around the fact that you went in my pocketbook while I was sleeping and charged up a bunch of shit on my card, I'm tryin to under..

"Vevee, there's no time for me to go into details about that. Listen, when I get out, I will be going into the city if you want to ride with me, we can discuss this all the way there and back.

Vevee stared at Dallen. His brow was furrowed and he looked her straight in the eye.

"I will call you when I get out, if you don't want to be bothered with me after you drop me off that's fine. Just give me a chance to be in my child's life if it is like you claim, my child."

"Damn him with his fine ass," Vevee stared at Dallen but couldn't speak.

He gathered up his belongings and kissed her on the cheek. She watched him walk out the door.

The waitress came over and Vevee ordered a hot tea. She called her sister Vindy and asked her to come down to the restaurant.

Vevee had to share her incredible story with someone. She couldn't hold it in any longer.

Chapter Twenty-Four

24.

Dallen

The paralegal called Dallen's cell phone before he reached the rental car. She wanted a credit card number or to verify he had cash and the extra fee of $1000.00 for short notice.

He assured her he had cash. He also stressed that he would be very appreciative of his immediate representation.

"The cops are pulling up behind me right now, lights and all," Dallen spoke to the women in a rushed tone.

"Please tell the attorney to meet me down at the station now. I think this lady may drop the charges."

Maybe not right away, Dallen thought to himself, but eventually she will.

Dallen took a deep breath and turned off his cell phone.

Chapter Twenty-five

25.

The Police

The police had followed Dallen from the parking lot. They confirmed it was the suspect that the credit card company had put a warrant out for. The officer was told to make sure he wasn't with or near the female acquaintance when they approached him.

Him and his partner agreed to wait until he left and meet him over at his car. That would create the least problem with the parking lot traffic and onlookers.

The 8 x 11 picture showed Dallen at the boutique on a cruise ship.

Although he had on sunglasses, the height, weight, and coloring looked like a match.

Since it was a fraud charge, the suspect shouldn't go ballistic and try and escape. He looked like he had some money and would just have to call his attorney to bail out.

They saw him exit the restaurant by himself so they slowly pulled behind his parked car and put on the flashers.

To be cont….

☐

A Sour Taste

A Sour Taste

Chapter One

The local club was half crowded and the music was very loud. The lights were dim, the bar ran along the wall to the left when you walked in, and to the right were 3 small round tables pushed up against a mirrored wall with two tall barstools on either side of the tables. When you walked past the end of the bar, the club opened up to more tables and chairs and a small dance floor. The DJ booth was in the right corner of the dance floor.

One couple sat at the bar with a few more men randomly seated. I could see straight past the bar to the back of the dance floor. He was over near the DJ's booth talking.

I know he saw me come in although now he was not even looking in my direction.

I sat down and ordered a martini. Halfway through my second martini my girlfriend showed up.

"Dead tonight huh? Oh, I see your boy in the back, did his wife make an appearance yet?"

Mina seemed to love to rub in the fact that he was married.

This didn't bother me because the one conversation I had with him, he expressed to me that he was not happy and not planning to stay that way for long.

"Not yet, but I'm sure she'll come flying in here after eight. She don't stay for long and he never pays her any mind so I don't know why she bothers."

"She just be trying to show off her working girl outfits and her latest weave," Mina said.

"Well, she ain't got nothing on me." I replied.

Mina got up to go speak to someone she knew and like a dream, he landed in the seat beside me.

His black mustache shined and his smooth skin matched the color of his chocolate brown shirt. Eye contact then my practiced killer smile did its work.

"Hi cutie, what's up?" He smiled as he talked showing pearly whites.

"Nothing much Trini, how you doin?" I said, trying to play it cool.

"I'm all right, I was talking to my boy and he was telling me about a party he's DJing at the Holiday Inn tomorrow night. Have you heard about it?" As he talked he constantly looked around. He nodded at certain women and looked back at the DJ booth every so often. His gold wedding band shined, but his black jeans was what I was checking out. They were hanging just the way I like them.

"Yeah, I thought it might be a lot of kids, why you going?" I could always make an exception if he was going to be there.

"I might step through there, it's 23 and over so it shouldn't be so bad." Trini said.

"Oh, yeah well as long as it won't be no little ruff necks in there jumping around I will surely check it out. You going to dance with me if I see you?" We made eye contact and I had his undivided attention for a minute until he checked the door and oh damn, in she came.

His wife made a beeline from the door to him and gave him a hug and a kiss mostly for my benefit I'm sure. Mina came switching right behind her, grinning.

"Uh-uh Trini, you in my seat," Mina swerved her hips and moved into Trini and his wife's space. His wife gave Mina the once over and stepped back.

Trini got up and moved towards the left side of the bar and ordered two drinks. His wife looked at me but didn't smile or speak. Trini got their drinks and they walked towards the DJ booth.

Mina didn't give me a chance to light my cigarette.

"What ya'll was talking about girl? He was sitting here for a while, I seen you smiling all the way from the juke box, and OOOH, how long was miss thing standing here with ya'll?," Mina was practically drooling, waiting for the details.

"We are going to the Holiday Inn tomorrow night so you better hit the mall tomorrow," I said.

"What? he invited you?" Mina looked at me like I was crazy.

"No, he didn't invite me, but he wants to meet me down there. It ain't like he can wine and dine me and take me out, but I know he wants to see me." A little exaggeration never hurt and I needed Mina to come with me there for moral support, in case his wife ended up tagging along with him.

"Well, I ain't got any plans; maybe he can hook me up with his DJ friend. You getting another drink?" Mina asked.

"No, after two I get a sour taste in my mouth."

Chapter Two

The next afternoon I was anxious worrying about what I should wear. I called Mina to see what she was wearing.

"Hey girl, I said, "What you doin?"

"My nails," she said.

"What you wearing tonight?" I asked.

"Black lace up the front shirt, red faded jeans, red boots," she said.

"Oh, you wearing jeans?, I'm gonna wear my black jeans so I could be comfortable." Mina knew she could work the hell out some jeans. I was originally going to wear a jean skirt but I didn't want Mina's curves to upstage mine.

I hadn't been out in a while to a real party aside from the local joint, I didn't want anything to go wrong.

"Whatever," she said, "I gotta finish my nails, so please get here early and bring your hair spray."

I pulled into the space in the front of the Mini-mall. It was still light out because I had to give us enough time to pick up the hairspray and drive the 45 minutes to the party.

As I was walking up to the store Trini and the DJ came walking out. Laughing and talking involved in conversation with another man.

Trini must have felt me starring because he turned his head slightly in my direction and caught my eye. He waved his hand and smiled. He was holding something, a prescription bottle maybe.

He said, "Hey cutie, see ya tonight."

Just then the DJ looked over his shoulder to see who Trini was speaking to and I could have swore he rolled his eyes at me. I just smiled back at Trini and waved. I didn't want to seem too desperate and yell a reply; I would save the conversation for later.

When I arrived at Mina's she was only half dressed. I sat on her overstuffed couch and fixed myself a drink.

"Girl, guess who I saw at the store," I said.

"Who?" Mina talked to me while she was curling her hair with a hot iron in the large bathroom off of her living area.

"Trini and the DJ and I could have swore the DJ rolled his eyes at me."

"Maybe he wants him for himself, he always up in his face and I don't never see him with no women."

The thought made me cringe.

"No," I said, "I think he is just friends with Trini's tag a long wife. Maybe they did the sneaky freaky, they all three always hanging tight."

"Maybe so," Mina replied.

The thought of Trini's wife being a nasty, freak of the week was comforting and went down smooth like my drink.

Chapter Three

We arrived late because of a delay with Mina's hairstyle. It took her at least an extra 30 minutes to get it together. We got there and it was mad packed.

I finished my drink and danced with a tall handsome stranger to Kanye and Jay Z. When I finished, I headed for a seat near the bar and ordered a soda. I heard "Hey cutie," in my right ear and turned to see a shiny black mustache and smooth brown skin, with dark sexy eyes staring into mine.

"Hi Trini," I said smiling.

"Lets dance," he offered.

"Sure," I said.

I followed him to the dance floor and had to tell myself to stop smiling.

I didn't want to look like a total jerk. Trini could dance and I couldn't help myself from checking his body out. The way his hips moved had me starring. He placed a firm hand on my waist and pulled me close. I could smell his King cologne. I moved like he moved so our bodies could touch. He smiled when I looked at him.

"You need to chill with me tonight girl," Trini whispered in my ear.

"We'll see about that." I tried to stop smiling so hard.

I wanted to play hard to get because I know I was looking hot. I turned around so he could check my look from the back.

I swayed my hips and bent my knees low and made sure my butt rubbed up against him when I danced and moved back to a standing position. I turned back around.

"You better stop playing with me," Trini warned in a playful way.

When the song stopped he took my hand and led me back to the seat near the bar. I thanked God for the empty seat next to mine. I felt like I was in high school, my stomach had major butterflies. He sat down and ordered us a beer.

"So you enjoying yourself?" he asked.

"Now that you're here."

Damn that beating around the bush, I wanted him bad and I wasn't playing the conservative sister any longer.

He put his hand on my thigh and said,

"You look real good tonight."

My skin burned under his touch. I licked my lips and looked into his eyes.

"So don't you," I replied, "Are you expecting your wife to show up tonight?" I asked.

"No, she wasn't feeling well so she took some medicine and it made her sleepy, so when I left she was laying down."

At that moment I noticed the prescription bottle in his top pocket.

"Why do you have medicine if she is the one who is sick?" I asked.

One thing I didn't want was a man on medication.

I could wait for whatever was ailing him to clear up. I wasn't that desperate.

"Oh, I gave her the pills before I left and instead of putting the bottle back I just put it in my pocket and forgot about it. These are some strong pills, she won't be needing no more tonight anyway," Trini explained.

Just then his DJ friend showed up.

"What's up Yvette," he said to me, giving me that same dry look Trini's wife always gave me.

"Trini can I talk to you for a minute?" he asked.

Trini finished his beer in a gulp, rubbed my arm and said,

"I'll be back later Yvette and maybe you'll give me another dance."

I smiled, I couldn't help it,

"O.K." I said, "Don't wait too long."

They took off towards the back.

Chapter Four

Mina appeared from the dance floor and I filled her in on the latest happenings.

"Whaaat?, she said, "You go girl."

About an hour passed before Trini came walking toward the bar, the DJ was hot on his trail. They didn't see me because I was on the dance floor. I tried not to stare in case Trini turned my way, but I couldn't help myself. I wanted to make sure he wasn't going to talk to the girl with the red mini at the bar staring at him. He got 2 drinks and gave one to the DJ. He put one on the bar and took out the prescription bottle from his top pocket.

People shifted around on the dance floor and when my view was clear again, he had both drinks in his hands and was walking back towards the corner of the room. My eyes followed him. Why would he take medication with liquor? was my first thought. But he said the prescription was for his wife. Why would he lie about that? Why did he order two drinks at one time? the DJ had one of his own. He didn't seem like the type to get totally drunk. My eye's continued to follow him to a table in the corner with a woman seated at it.

He gave her the drink but it was hard to see who she was. They were too far away and the lights were very low.

When I finished dancing I found Mina and made her walk around the room and nonchalantly glance back at the corner Trini was in with his mystery date and the DJ.

To my total surprise it was his wife. My
stomach felt like I swallowed a bowling ball.
I got stiff and couldn't turn around to see if
Trini looked as disgusted by her presence as
I felt. Mina took my arm after reading my
facial expression, we headed for the bar. I
needed a drink bad.

"Well girl, you better make other plans for
tonight." Mina said.

"I know," was all I could manage to get out.
I wanted to actually cry.

Chapter Five

I sat and tried to drown my sorrows but I
really didn't have enough money to do that.
So I sat and watched everyone for a while. I
saw the DJ come back to the bar twice to get
drinks. When I finally worked up the nerve
to look in that corner, all three of them were
sitting there laughing and talking. Why
didn't the DJ ever have a date? I wondered.
I bet they were some sort of freaky
threesome. That thought made me feel a
little better. Maybe Trini wasn't my type
after all.

The night was almost over and I went
outside to smoke.

No one was outside yet, it was quiet. The cool air felt good and my head started to clear.

I heard a door open and loud talking and laughter. I looked around to see where it was coming from. Out the side door that leads to the parking lot, people were leaving. I decided this was a good spot for me to see who was creeping out the club since it wasn't going to be me. The cement bench I was sitting on was hidden by a huge planter in front of me. The look was very contemporary but not comfortable at all. The exit to the main street from the parking lot was at the far end in the other direction so people leaving didn't have to drive by me.

I saw another couple leaving, the girl in the red mini and Mina's ex who was very noticeable in white jeans and very married. Wait until I tell Mina, I thought.

Now the side exit had my full attention, this was beginning to be fun. I lit another cigarette.

Chapter Six

Next came Trini, his wife and the DJ. Trini
was holding her arm on one side and the DJ
was holding the other arm. She stumbled to
her car. I know they are not going to let her
drive, I thought to myself. Oh yes they
were, I could see as they opened the driver's
door and sort of lead, sort of shoved her into
the driver's seat.

She put her head back against the head rest
and I thought good, they are going to let her
sleep. Trini reached over her and started the
car, let the window down on the drivers'
side and closed the door. Then he leaned
into the car window and it looked like he
was talking to her, maybe he kissed her.

Trini and the DJ stepped back and the wife drove off real fast, swerving. Oh well, I thought, maybe she can drunk drive better than I think. Trini and the DJ started to walk towards me and I thought I would be busted. Instead they stopped at Trini's black four by four and got in. I turned myself to make sure they couldn't see me. I figured I would wait until they drove off before I would head back inside.

They sat talking and then the DJ leaned over and kissed Trini square on the mouth.

It seemed to me that the kiss lasted almost as long as I had a crush on Trini, almost as long as I had fantasized about us being together. I almost screamed. I sat stiff and shocked until they drove off.

Chapter Seven

A few days later the police came to question
me about the night of the Holiday Inn party.
Trini's wife was killed in a car accident and
they wanted to question me about the
conversation I had with Trini at the party.
The autopsy revealed a high dose of
prescription drugs mixed with alcohol in her
system. Trini told the police that he didn't
see his wife at the party and danced with me
several times. He told them we even
discussed her condition and how he left her
at home resting. The DJ's statement said
that he told Trini he saw his wife outside the
party drunk, but by the time Trini made it
out there to see her, she had already pulled
off.

I thought back on the dry ass look his wife always gave me, then I smiled at the officer and agreed with everything Trini had told him.

The crowd at the local bar is a lot younger now-a-days. I heard Trini moved out of town and the bar is looking for a new DJ.

◻

226

The Back Stairs

Forward

The Back Stairs

I wrote this short story for everyone who is
on the grind and stays on the grind. When I
say the grind I mean the J. O. B. This is for
everyone, especially the Sisters who hold it
down and have been holdin it down. This is
for all my men and women who have been
working since they were about 15 years old,
like me. All who have been dealing with
different relationships on the job,
overlooking certain things, and turning the
other cheek, and holding your tongue. This
is even for all of you who don't or won't or
can't hold their tongue and had to go find
another job because of it.

This is for all of you who have to show up to somewhere you especially don't want to be to hit 40 hours and get that check. Regardless of how much crap their dishing out, sometimes you just gotta show up and get your money. I want to say to you all to keep on keeping on. You can't be held back if you focus on your goal. Your job may be short term or temporary. If it's not the perfect job for you, set a goal to move on and go for it. If I can do it, so can't you.

"I can do all things through Christ which strengths me." Philippians 4:13. Cruisin' and Other Short Stories is about relationships. **The Back Stairs** is about a work relationship that takes an unexpected turn. I hope you enjoy it.

The Back Stairs

Chapter 1.

Her husband rested his hand on her hips. No longer was there a soft roundness but an angle. Her body was becoming more athletic.

"Babe," he nudged her, "time to rise and shine."

Lauren sat up on the edge of the bed. Her husband had walked into the adjoining bathroom in the spacious master suite. She heard the water to the shower start up. Walking towards the chaise lounge where her sweat suit was thrown from the day before, Lauren pulled on the bottoms and took off her nightshirt.

After washing her face and brushing her teeth she started out to her morning workout.

Lauren took a deep breath of the fresh morning air. Fall was near, Lauren welcome the change in weather. Connecticut's humid summers could wear you down.

"My hair won't frizz today," she thought to herself as she headed down the tree lined driveway.

She stopped and stretched before running onto the main streets sidewalk. Lauren's street as well as the next one over was a cul-de-sac. Both streets ran off a main drive. Luckily for Lauren, a sidewalk ran along her street, down the main drive and onto the cul-de-sac one street over.

4 times a week Lauren ran up and around completing an even 2 mile run.

Over the past 8 months she had lost almost 20 pounds. Lauren looked and felt great.

Lauren admired the color of her new Lexus truck as she walked back towards her home in cool down mode. Inside she showered and changed into a comfortable pant suit. Lauren packed a bag of fruit and munchies for her long day at the office.

As she took the short drive in to work, she thought back a couple of months to the changes that had recently occurred in her life. A promotion came when she least expected it. A position opened up at a company she had interviewed for months before. Lauren had long given up on it, but never stopped praying for something better. All her hard work and praying to the Lord had finally paid off.

Her commute would be 35 minutes each way. This was a change from her usual 15 minute ride in. Lauren looked forward to spending the extra time in her new truck. The last two weeks of work were turning out great. Lauren's boss left on vacation for a week giving her plenty of time to tie up loose ends without anyone breathing down her neck.

Pulling into a prime parking spot that she lucked up on, she was feeling good. Lauren's mood changed when she headed to the entrance door of her job. The thought of passing by the security desk caused her stomach to have butterflies.

"If he says something, I'm saying something back," Lauren thought to herself.

She rarely said anything at all to the guard except "Good morning." Most days, if she felt like it, she would add a smile while she spoke. Although she heard his off color compliments, usually she kept quiet and ignored him.

Lately his comments were more direct. Two weeks ago when she was passing by the security guard said something like

"Hey Laura, girl you look good, and I bet you smell good to."

Lauren ignored him.

This morning when she passed by he stared hard at her then said,

"Hey Laura, those pants are fitting nice, you must have lost about 40 or 50 pounds."

Lauren stopped in her tracks. She looked around to see if anyone else heard but the hallway was empty. The guard stared at her grinning.

The comment pissed her off for 3 reasons. First she had just weighed herself and confirmed that she had just dropped another 10 pounds making her total weight loss close to 20 pounds. It was hard work on her part and Lauren was proud of herself. Him guessing such a high number hurt her feelings.

2nd she didn't appreciate the way he felt so comfortable boldly staring at her ass every time she walked by. Lauren could see his reflection in the glass of the windows she passed and he didn't even try to hide the fact that he would watch her until she hit the door to the stairway.

3rd she had told him at least twice that her name was Not Laura.

"Yes," Lauren turned to address him, "I did lose some weight, but it was hardly 40 pounds. I wasn't that big. It seems to me you should be paying closer attention to your own weight, and stop worrying about mine."

Lauren was letting it out and it felt good so she continued. He was catching years of her built up frustration from all of the unwanted glares, stares, and sleazy comments.

She was sick and tired of ignoring him and others like him, men and lately women to with their bold advances and unwanted come ons.

Lauren knew that over time these comments were affecting her and her self image. She thought back to the shopping spree her and her girlfriend went on celebrating her new job. Lauren steered away from a pant suit she tried on.

Although her girlfriend insisted it fit cute and encouraged her to show off her new lean figure, Lauren put it back. She felt it was too tight and didn't want anyone

staring at her backside at work. On the drive home she regretted putting the suit back.

Her girlfriend commented

"My creepy co-workers can stare at my ass all they want, they can plant a big wet one on it to!"

They laughed loudly at that on the ride home.

Lauren continued to give the guard attitude.

"I'm not sure if you're just slow or hard of hearing, but I told you before, my name is not Laura. So I won't have to correct you again, you can just save all your little comments to yourself and don't say shit to me."

With that Lauren started back to the stairs and didn't turn back.

Chapter 2.

"Take that back!" the security guard yelled. "Don't talk to me like that."

The security guard stood up from behind his station, yelling at Lauren's back while she went through the door to the back stairwell.

He stared at her and waited for her to turn back around. He watched the stairwell door close. He sat back down in his chair staring in disbelief.

"What the hell was wrong with her?" the guard thought to himself.

"Every time I try and be nice to one of these stuck up witches, it backfires. Can't anyone recognize a compliment anymore?"

Since no one was in the hallway to hear the exchange between the two, the guard's ego was spared for the most part.

"I'll make sure I won't say nothing to her, next time I see her I'm gonna act like I don't see her."

The guard looked down at his gut hanging over his belt and thought about what she said.

"I got to see her every day, and one day she's gonna need me to open the door, or help her carry something in, or something" the guard mumbled to himself.

The guard thought of the last time he passed her in the stairwell and he held the door open for her because her hands were full. He thought she smiled at him extra long.

A tall thin woman passed by the guard's desk and put his mind back on his job. He smiled at the women but she passed by without acknowledging him.

"Women," the guard thought to himself, "always playing hard to get. They know what they really want."

He shook his head and went back to checking employees work ID's.

Chapter 3

Lauren laughed to her co-worker while she repeated the story for the 3rd time that day.

"Girl, you should have seen his face. I think he stood up and for a minute I thought he was gonna run after me."

Lauren laughed harder along with her co-worker.

"But Lauren," her co-worker started,

"I heard he goes off sometime."

She moved from standing in front of the microwave in the lounge to sitting down at one of the little square tables.

She placed her microwave lunch in front of her and peeled the plastic film the rest of the way off.

"Yeah, she continued, "I heard he was sort of stalking this lady and one day confronted her in the back stairwell, you know the stairs you take. Anyway, the lady slapped the crap out of him first because of whatever he said to her, but then he grabbed her by the neck and was choking her."

"What?!"

Lauren interrupted her co-worker trying to process the unbelievable story.

"Are you serious?"

"Yes Girl," her co-worker continued,

"The cameras caught it all. That lady left the job and never pressed charges they say.

So they kinda made it seem like he was in a relationship with her or whatever."

"What the heck is he still doing here working?" Lauren asked her coworker in horror.

"Well the lady smacked him first and I guess she had her own on the job issues so they made it seem like she was just as crazy. Girl you know it's who you know up in here. Maybe he knew someone that let him keep his job."

Lauren sat at her desk for the next hour and waited till it was time to leave. Regret for how she reacted with the guard started to set in. She pushed the slight feeling of fear away and tried to think about her new job.

Lauren also felt sort of good for standing up for herself. She was not the only women tired of the guard's comments.

She remembered how he made her feel nervous or self conscious when she passed by.

She remembered conversations she had with co-workers after they suggested using the other entrance because of his bold comments and how they all agreed it was inappropriate.

"I only got a few more days here, I can do this."

Lauren made up her mind not to let the security guard ruin the last couple of days at the job. She thought momentarily about bringing a weapon to protect herself. Lauren wondered "But what would I bring?"

Leaving work for the day she took the front elevator and walked outside around to the back lot where her car was, avoiding the security desk.

On her way home she drove by the local community center and saw classes advertised on the sign near the intersection. They were offering self defense classes starting that night.

Lauren went home, changed her clothes and headed back to the community center.

The class was $40 dollars and the instructor was fine.

Lauren paid her money and waited in the gym with the other 5 women and one other man who signed up also.

The instructor took them through a series of 10 steps over and over for about 2 hours. A 20 minute break was given for bathroom and water.

At the end of the class Lauren was impressed with herself. She went home and talked her husband into letting her practice her moves on him.

Lauren was able to drop her husband to his knees and have him in a head lock within a 3 minute struggle.

Of course she didn't knee her husband in the groin like they were instructed to do, but he understood the process.

"All right Baby, Im'a have you come to my job and kick this man's butt for me. He keeps parking in my spot" her husband teased.

"But seriously, I think what you learned is well worth your $40 dollars."

Lauren's husband went to bed.

Lauren stayed up and practiced more. She didn't tell her husband about the security guard. She didn't want to blow things out of proportion and give him need to worry. She would be leaving the job for good in a few days and it hardly seemed right to bother him.

Especially since her class, she felt she could handle herself and anything that came her way.

Chapter 4

Lauren's next couple of days at work went by uneventfully. She went her old route to her office and walked by the security desk to the stairs; the guard didn't acknowledge her or even look her way.

Lauren was relieved.

"I guess he learned who to talk shit to and who to leave the hell alone," Lauren thought to herself.

Chapter 5

The next day was her last day there, her last Friday. She knew her last day she would have to carry a box of her stuff to her car. She knew she would have to take the back stairs. The thought unnerved her a little, but the last time she passed the security desk, there was a different guard sitting there. Having worked in the same building for a while, Lauren knew that sometimes the guards were rotated to different posts. She felt some of her anxiety subside. Maybe her last day would be just as good as her first.

Lauren enjoyed the party her department threw for her. She ate too much cake and said her goodbyes to co-workers she knew she would never see again. Lauren waited until the end of the day to back up her box.

Lauren thought to herself,

"Ill run this last report and leave half day."

Chapter 6

Lauren's last day didn't go exactly how she planned it. The computer was down for most of the morning. Her boss asked her to stay and run the report they were depending on her to run.

Reluctantly, Lauren stayed.

On her way to leave her plants in her car, she noticed the guard she was avoiding sitting back at the security desk. He looked at her but didn't say anything; she looked at him and quickly looked away.

"Damn" she thought to herself, "I hope he doesn't know this is my last day." Lauren felt the butterfly's in her stomach.

Even though it was Lauren last day, she didn't want to see the man who caused her discomfort and anxiety.

She was already annoyed because she had to cancel the lunch she had planned with her friends because she had to stay late and run the report her boss requested.

The computers came back up late afternoon. Lauren had finished packing her desk and training the girl who was going to temporarily fill her spot. She showed her how to run the reports.

"Do you want me to help carry your stuff out Lauren?" her coworker asked her while sizing up the box in the corner and a bag with a few nick nacks and pictures stuffed in it.

"Nah, I got it," Lauren answered.

She didn't want to ask for help, she figured she could grab all of it in one trip and possibly leave at least an hour early. She didn't need her coworker questioning her.

The clock struck 4:00 and Lauren put her pocketbook on top of the already full box. She took one look around her cubicle and grabbed the box with both hands.

It was a little heavier than she anticipated. She set the box down and got out her car keys. Lauren picked back up the box, grabbed her keys that were on her desk, and looked at the bag sitting on the chair in the corner.

Lauren put the box back down on the desk. She put her keys back in her pocketbook. She figured she would set her box down outside the car when she reached it, then she would fish her keys out of her pocketbook. Just then she remembered she left her car door unlocked when she brought the plants out earlier, so she wouldn't have to worry about digging out keys.

She would use her few extra fingers to grab
the bag on the chair and maneuver her way
down the back stairs.

Chapter 7

"I should have brought this bag down when I took the plant to my car."

Lauren was feeling frustrated that the box was a little harder to manage along with the bag that was strangling her fingers. Lauren used her fingers to turn the door handle just enough and leaned hard into it.

The door opened to the back stairs.

Down one flight of stairs Lauren could look over the banister and see the door to the stairwell open from below. She had two more sets of stairs to navigate down.

She heard footsteps coming up but couldn't see due to the fact her pocket book sitting on top of the box was blocking much of her view. Lauren slowed down a little but kept going down the stairs.

Standing on the landing Lauren adjusted the bag strangling her fingers. She could see the last flight of 4 stairs she had to go down, she could also see the guard she was avoiding coming up the stairs.

He met her on the landing and looked over her pocketbook in her eyes.

"Moving out?" the guard asked while he smiled at Lauren.

Lauren panicked and tried to step quickly around him.

The sudden movement jerked her pocketbook hobbling on top of her box causing it to slid off and hit the stairs, it bounced down the steps and landed right in front of the exit door. Both Lauren and the guard looked at it.

Lauren started down the last few stairs without replying to the guard. This made him very angry.

"Hey," he said, "let me get that for you."

The guard rushed down the steps by her and grabbed her pocketbook from the ground. He stood in front of the door holding it out to her.

"Thanks" Lauren said, "Can you please just put it on top of my box?"

Lauren held the box away from her face in front of the guard. She wanted to grab her pocketbook from him but she would have had to put the box down.

"I knew you would need me," the guard said while he stood in front of the door.

Lauren just looked at him and he stared back.

"I asked you were you moving," the guard said.

"Yeah," Lauren replied.

She tried to keep her voice calm and not let her annoyance show.

"Where you going?"

The Guard questioned her while still holding her pocketbook.

"I'm in sort of a rush," Lauren refused to hold a conversation with him.

"Can you please just give me my pocketbook?"

"Well where are you going in such a rush?" the Guard asked.

"I knew you would need me," the Guard repeated for the second time. This time Lauren was the one who got angry.

"I don't need you, but you need to give me my damn pocketbook."

Lauren was looking down from the third step at the guard who was still standing in front of the door.

 Although he was thick, Lauren had the urge to kick him in his chest and throw the box at him. When the guard didn't reply to her, she felt the tension growing between them and decided to get out of the stairwell.

She started down the last couple of steps towards him and the door.

"Really," Lauren started, "You can just leave my pocketbook on the step, I'm just rushing to my car to load this box and I'm coming right back."

Lauren reached the last step and reached for the door handle, using the box as a barrier between them, she felt the box bump into his arm while he tried not to move out of her way.

The guard used his big black boot to close the exit door. This scared Lauren.

No more talking she thought.

She turned to him and looked down at his foot and then back at his face. He had a serious expression.

"O.K," Lauren thought to herself, "It's on." Lauren turned her back to him. She put the box down on the stairs and thought about running up a flight to the next exit door. But she didn't.

Lauren decided to stand up for herself. She looked the guard dead in his eye.

He had a slightly confused look as he looked at her then back to the box on the stairs. Certainly he didn't expect her to turn boldly to him like she was.

"So what do you want to do?" she questioned him.

Before he could answer Lauren snatched the pocketbook from his hand.

The guard took a step back with a surprised look on his face, and then went for her neck with both hands. Lauren stepped back this time and backed into the box that was sitting on the stairs. Her weight tipped it over and all her little desk accessories spilled out.

She could feel him pulling her towards him by the neck. She dropped the bag she was holding.

Lauren remembered her self defense class and the moves she had practiced. She let herself be pulled up into to his chest and kneed him in the groin as hard as she could. As the Guard gasped and kneeled down on one knee she slapped him hard across the right cheek and let her nail scratch the side of his face near his ear. The guard gasped and leaned back into the wall.

His surprised look, followed by confused stare, he looked at Lauren like she was something he never saw before.

Quickly Lauren opened the door and leaned on it while grabbing the box on the stairs and her bag. She had to leave a few items that spilled out behind; her favorite stapler was right near where the guard was kneeling. Standing over him she couldn't fight the urge to kick him so she did… Hard in the stomach. He grabbed for her leg but she was out the door.

Lauren ran to her car, threw everything in the backseat and took off out the parking lot at top speed.

Chapter 8

When Lauren got home she immediately told her husband what had transpired between her and the guard. Her husband's first reaction was to get in the car and go back to her job.

Lauren talked him out of it. Reasoning that if he was still there, which she doubted considering the time, things would escalate and the guard was hardly worth any legal trouble. After some convincing, her husband calmed down. Lauren managed to make it into more of a joke, and assured her husband she had the upper hand when it came to the struggle.

Her husband was not hearing any of it. He grabbed his coat and wallet and yelled for Lauren to come on.

With his face and his voice serious, Lauren knew not to argue with her husband. They rode in silence at top speed to the police station.

After waiting twenty minutes to be seen, a police officer listened to her story and filed charges against the security guard. The police officer explained to Lauren and her Husband that she must put the same complaint in at the job, even if she didn't work there anymore. They assured them that an officer would get the guards address from the job and someone would go by to serve a warrant.

Lauren promised her husband she would call the security office and report what happened. Then if they needed to return to place charges or whatever, she would let her husband know and he could accompany her.

At her husband's urging, Lauren called the security office when they got back home. After 5 minutes of voicemail prompts, she reached the security office. The security officer informed her that particular guard had left for the day but the incident would be logged and reviewed by his supervisor. He told her if she wanted to press charges she would have to go through the local police department.

Lauren explained that she already had been to the Police department.

Lauren left her cell phone number for the security office to reach her and tried to forget about it and relax. Before she got to comfortable her cell phone rang. The security officer on the other end was the district manager in charge of all the security staff in that building. He asked her to repeat her story and asked about witnesses.

He said since there were no witnesses, he would have to review the tape along with a police officer. He would send her a formal complaint form and asked that she fax or e-mail it back asap. The security officer promised he would follow up with her 1st thing on Monday.

After explaining to the officer that she would not be returning to that building because it was her last day, they agreed to touch base with each other through phone calls.

Chapter 9

After a relaxing weekend, Lauren felt
refreshed and rejuvenated for her new job.
She carried with her a new sense of self and
confidence. She was not scared of many
things before the incident with the Guard,
but now she was fearless.

Her 1st day on the job went by fast. She
filled out initial HR paperwork and found
her way around her new surroundings. She
had a much bigger cubicle space and
enjoyed the faster paced more modern office
environment.

Many of her coworkers where around her
age or younger, she felt the space for growth
here.

Lauren had almost forgot about the incident that took place that past Friday until she checked her voicemail messages on her cell phone.

"Ms. James, this is officer Tiptop from the BS security office. I am calling to tell you we reviewed the video tapes and although we could not see that actual altercation because of where you two were standing, we did view you enter the stairwell, the accused officer enter the stairwell and you fleeing from the stairwell.

We also were able to view spilled contents from your box as you described and the slightly bruised guard exiting the stairwell soon after you."

"The fact that the accused security officer did not show up for work today and did not call probably means he was involved in some sort of altercation with you.

We are taking your word for what happened, because this is not the first complaint we have against this guard."

After calling the security officer back, he explained to Lauren that she had made a formal complaint but still needed to meet with the police to follow up if she chooses to. A warrant had been issued through the police department, but it was just for questioning because she couldn't prove the assault. If the guard returned to that job, he would be immediately dismissed and police would be notified. They did not need any more information from her and were considering the case closed. He apologized for what she experienced and left his number if she ever needed his help.

Lauren felt somewhat relieved after their conversation and decided to talk to her husband.

Lauren no longer felt intimated so she didn't really want to spend anymore of her time on what she considered a non-issue.

Later that evening Lauren and her husband went out to dinner. It was their favorite spot and the food was always fresh and the service good. They spent a short time discussing her next steps regarding the altercation she had. After some reassuring, her husband agreed they probably wouldn't hear from Mr. Security guard anymore. Since she had a new job neither of them would worry about her running into him.

Lauren looked down at her fingernail she had to file down after she broke it scratching the guards face.

"I'll get this fixed tomorrow after work and that will be the last reminder of this horrible experience," Lauren told her husband.

They talked about advocating for the self defense courses for their nieces and other females they knew could benefit.

The evening ended on a positive note.

Chapter 10

The security guard sat on his couch with a cold beer watching his 13 inch T.V. He ran his finger along the scratch on the right side of his cheek near his ear. He couldn't believe the turn of events over the last 48 hours. The Guard didn't worry about the Police coming to look for him. The address the security office had was 2 years old. He had moved 3 times since then.

He quit his job and for the first time in a long time felt old and a little scared of his surroundings. The Guard was use to being the intimidator, especially when it came to women.

He didn't want to job hunt and knew it would be difficult finding yet another security gig. The warning he got from the last incident at work still rang fresh in his ears.

The guard got up from his couch and walked the short way into his kitchenette to get another beer. Passing the counter he glanced at the card he had picked up from the stairwell after his altercation with the women.

The card read a company name and address he recognized as an advertising company down the interstate, maybe 40 or so minutes away. The rest of the pens and stapler he threw in the garbage. On his way back to the couch he vowed to look up this company and check the staff names. He knew, or at least he thought the woman he fought with name was Laura something or other. How many Laura's could be at one place at one time?

The thought of tracking her down made him tired. He put his feet up and contemplated his options.

He would go down to the employment office first thing Monday morning.

"I could forget about her and move on," he thought to himself. "She ain't worth no trouble."

The guard put the cold beer against his cheek.

"Maybe I'll forget about it," he thought, to himself, "and maybe I won't."

The guard let the cold beer sooth the still sore scratch on his cheek.

Final Chapter

Lauren was enjoying her commute more and more each day. She found an inexpensive coffee shop on her way in and often stopped. She found herself exploring her new surroundings and stopping at the different boutiques she passed.

Today she noticed the same white car that was behind her yesterday, behind her today. She tried not to be paranoid. Lauren had barely thought about the incident at

her old job at all.

Today, looking in her rearview, she thought about it.

☐

Reading Group

Questions for discussion

1. Cruisin'

A. Does Dallen have a good side to him?

B. Does he have potential or is he too old to change his ways?

C. Is Vevee to trusting? Naïve?

D. What made Vevee go back even though she saw red flags?

E. Would parenting a child be a realistic option for Dallen and Vevee?

F. Were Vevee's standards for
dating in tune with today's
working class single woman?

2. A Sour Taste

A. Was Mina a good friend to Yvette?

B. Was the information Yvette held from the police relevant to their investigation?

C. People leading double lives. Is this a real topic of concern or just a juicy fiction storyline?

3. The Back Stairs

A. Who do you know that would have stood up for herself like Lauren?

B. Are women victims because of their work environments more than men?

C. Do you think Lauren should have bought a weapon or a deterrent like pepper spray to work? Why or why not?

D. Are you prepared to defend yourself in a critical situation?

If you enjoyed the stories in this book, look

out for Dianne Gill's next book with the

continuing saga of Vevee and Dallen and

more from Lauren and her office

relationships. Go to the website at:

www.djamespublishingllc.com

for news on release dates and to pre-order.

end